I0679087

Desire's Shadow

By

Gina Camp

Published by
GC Ink Publications LLC
P.O. Box 59279
Pittsburgh, PA. 15210

This book is a work of fiction. Names, characters, places and incidents are products of the author's imagination or are used fictitiously. Any resemblance to actual events or locales or persons, living or dead, is entirely coincidental.

All rights reserved. No part of this book may be reproduced in any form or by any means, without the prior written consent of the Publisher, excepting brief quotes used in reviews.

For permissions, interviews, bookings or other information, contact GC Ink at gc.inkpublications@gmail.com
Like our Facebook page at www.facebook.com/gcinkpublications

Copyright © 2013

ISBN 978-0-9913053-0-8 pbk
ISBN 978-0-9913053-1-5 ebook

Printed in United States of America

Acknowledgments

I've been blessed with a gift and I am truly thankful to the creator who bestowed it upon me. Forever humble and grateful for each day and each moment I am given on this earth, I am determined not to take one second, nor the things and people that mean the most to me for granted.

First and foremost, I'd like to thank my husband and children for riding with me while I took the plunge and followed my book writing journey, encouraging me along the way. Things like, "So babe, how much did you get done today?" was enough to make me stay focused so I could have something to share when asked. "Mom, is your book done?" was motivation enough for me to keep going until I finished what I started. I am blessed to have you guys in my life and it helps that we are close, loving and supportive of one another.

To my Mom, my #1 Fan and Cheerleader – I did it!!! I know you're saying, "Finally!" Thank you for always being there for me and cheering me on even as I kept failing to Get A MOVE On It! I Love You Thiiiiiiiiiiiiiiiiiiiiiiiiiiiiiiiiiiiiiiiiiiiiiiiiiiiis Much and More!!! – No more writings in the drawer. ☺

To my siblings, thank you all for your encouragement and support. I may be the oldest, but it means a lot to me to hear you say how proud you are of my accomplishments and to know "Yall got my Back" – I Love You All to Pieces!!!! Malcolm, you have been more than a brother – you've been a consultant, mentor and friend. Thanks Michael and Kierstin (and my cousin Larry) for being good sports and allowing me to use your photos for my 'special' cover. Consider yourselves as having famous faces because I'm going to push this thing until it's a #1 Best Seller in the hands and on the bookshelves of millions. ☺ Cousin Larry, a.k.a. Skip – you already know!!... I love you and thanks for all your support!

To my cousin Mikala and friend's Jenea and Tameka – I thank you ladies from the bottom of my heart for letting me call you up many, many times and run my ideas and thoughts by you and for sharing your feedback with me. Kala, you always make me feel like I'm the sh*t – lol!! You are no doubt the best person to have at my side, especially when it comes to promotions ☺ – I am grateful to have such love and support as genuine as yours! Love Ya!! Jenea – your questions and always wanting more really kept me going. You had me cracking up throughout this whole process and you're excitement about it really kept me feeling enthusiastic to get it done. Tameka, Girl – You are the BEST!!! I appreciate you taking the time to read my book and give me notes, chapter by chapter, all while being a busy lady. You always lend your ear, no matter the situation and I thank you for that. Kudos for being such a wonderful person – Always!

Hadji, Hadji, Hadji – I just love your name – lol! So much so that the day you walked into the office – I told you I wanted to use it for a character in my book. Thanks for the green light... I think he's going to be a lot of ladies' favorite character. You've been so supportive ever since and I appreciate my new, forever friend that I have in you.

Last, but not least, I'd like to thank my Family and Friends who been with me from the start. It was you who encouraged me along the way, constantly telling me how great of a writer I am. From reading my works, attending my performances on down to constantly asking "When you gonna write that book?", "You still writing?" and "Can I have a copy of that poem you wrote?" - All those things helped to groom me for this accomplishment – you guys have been instrumental in keeping me motivated. I finally did it and I hope you enjoy. Love Always!!! – Gina (Bambina to some ☺)

MAD Styles

M.A.D. Styles
412-623-7899 (412- MAD STYL)
MaKenzie A. Dixon – Owner/Stylist
Offers Full-Service Hair, Nail, Skin & Body Bar

Hours: Tuesday - Saturday 9 a.m. - 9 p.m.
Mondays and after 9 pm: By Appointment Only

Barbers:	Stylists:
Greg, Julian	Selena, Bella
Lanel	Carmen

Nail Technician – Nitra ... by appointment only!

Nitra

I got to the shop around eight-fifteen. MaKenzie, the owner, was already there. She was in her office on her cell phone when I came in. We smiled and waved at each other while she continued on with her conversation. I pulled her door shut lightly as I made my way to turn on the music. Juke must have been the last person to leave last night because as soon as I pressed play, Waka Flocka's "No Hands" came blazing through the speakers. I quickly turned it down and then turned it off to find something more suitable to *my* liking since I was the first worker there. Julian, nickname – Juke, was the youngest of the three barbers who worked there and I was the youngest amongst the ladies. His choice in music showed his age – mine didn't. I am a tender twenty-two years old described as having an old soul. Juke was MaKenzie's twenty year old nephew whom she took care of since he was thirteen. Her sister, Roxie, was *and still is* strung out on drugs and Makenzie didn't want her only nephew to get caught up in the streets. After high school, she promised him a job at the shop and a car if he got his barber's license. He followed through by attending and graduating from Barber School and as promised she gave him a job and bought the boy a Camaro. Must be nice!

Carmen and Bella came through the door as I shuffled through the pile of cd's and settled on a new school R&B mix. "Hey Nitra," they said almost in unison, greeting me as they made their way to their stations. They are friends outside the shop and are often together when they aren't at work. They are a little older than I and treated me more like a little sister rather than their peer.

Carmen and the other stylist, Selena, tolerated each other for the sake of business, but weren't too fond of each other when they figured out they were doing the same guy. He wasn't claiming either one of them - which I guess is what kept them from throwing blows. They were both still fighting for that number one spot, so for the moment they would both play their position. It would only be a matter of time before that situation blows up and I'm going to have front row seats to the show.

Bella kept it real at all times and was cool with every damn body. She didn't treat Selena any different than anyone else just because she and Carmen didn't like each other. "She hasn't done anything to *me*," She would say every time Carmen expected her to choose sides. Bella spoke her mind – tactfully, and is not the tell- you-what-you-want-to-hear type. She always says, "I call it like I see it." Carmen got some shit with her and Bella called her on it every time.

I've been working at M.A.D. Styles for the past year and four months today, and it has become my home away from home. Since June 11ᵗʰ of last year to be exact and I am totally comfortable here. I love the atmosphere and the ambiance is off the chain. I get along well with everybody and it didn't take long for them to treat me more like family than anything else. *I tend to have that effect on people. Hey, I'm a people person!*

MaKenzie's husband has plenty money and put a lot into making his wife's dream a reality, exactly as she envisioned it. MaKenzie is twenty-eight, spunky, yet private about the details of the goings on in her life – with everyone except me. I am like a little sister to her is what she says.

Her office was a mini-shop in itself. A huge mahogany desk with a glass top sat to the left as you walked in. She had a plush burgundy and black chair with a matching footstool that she used when she wanted to relax in between customers. She provided full service to her clients, right from her "office" – able to do their manis & pedis, apply lashes, arch or wax eyebrows, cut, style or color their hair and whatever else they needed – on down to applying their make-up and giving massages and facials. Everything she needed to perform all of her duties was in her mini-shop of an office. It was spacious, yet cozy and she had the nerve to have her own personal bathroom, complete with a shower.

She basically let us do our own thing while she did hers. She could see what was going on anyway because the monitors to the security system were also located in there with her. Interesting enough – no one knew where the cameras were located. If you looked around, you saw no cameras on the walls or ceilings and no one has ever noticed any flashing, nor steady red lights indicating there was an alarm. I'd say it was a genius idea to have the system set up so inconspicuous. People tend to forget they are being watched up in here. Out of sight, out of mind, I guess.

Greg, the oldest of the barbers, came in at ten to nine. We spoke as he headed straight for MaKenzie's office and knocked on the door. "She here," he asked neither one of us in particular. Before anyone could respond, Kenzie opened the door, signaling with her index finger for him to give her a minute. "She still on that phone," I thought to myself. "That must be some serious business."

She finished up her call, came out of her office and talked to him while she shuffled through some papers at the front desk.

Greg was usually the last to leave because he doubled as the cleaning guy to make some extra money. He figured why let them pay someone else when he was right there all the time. Plus, he had no wife or kids, or a girlfriend for that matter, so why not make some extra paper in his spare time.

I heard him telling MaKenzie that he got another nighttime job but wanted to refer a friend of his who owned his own cleaning company to take over.

"I'm going to have to talk to my husband first and see what he wants to do. You know how Reese is. He doesn't trust just anybody. Do I know this cat – he been here before?" MaKenzie asked.

"Yea, he comes through every now and then. I put my name on him Kenzie; I wouldn't recommend anyone I didn't trust. This place is my bread and butter. Plus I think Reese might be familiar with him already, but here's his card in case yall interested. And uh, I need the rest of the day off if you don't

8

mind. I don't have any appointments scheduled so I was hoping it wouldn't be a problem."

MaKenzie shook her head no while still looking down. "Mmhm. No problem. Sure. No, I don't mind," she said, sounding and looking like she was listening but really not. She must be in a damn good mood today and that call must have been a good one because she is zoned out.

"You got some time to square up right now then?" he asked. "I need that cash for a date I got tonight." A big grin spread across his face.

"A date? Ok playa! Yea, I have time," MaKenzie said, finally looking up from the desk to see the giddy expression on Greg's face. We all laughed and hit him with the "Woooo".

Bella said, "Who is she Greg and when the crew get to meet her?"

"We'll see how tonight goes and then I'll know what's up. I'm hoping it doesn't turn out to be a scene from "Hell Date" or no shit. It's a blind date. I don't know what she's like yet."

Carmen said, "Awe shit, call us if you need us. This could get interesting. I got a feeling you going to have us cracking the hell up when we hear this one. Matter of fact," she took one of her business cards out the holder at her station and walked over to hand it to Greg, "Take this, my cell number is on there. Call me as soon as it's over." We all laughed.

"Carmen, do I look like one of your gossiping girlfriends?" He shook his head, putting her card in his pocket.

He and MaKenzie went in her office and handled their business. It was time to get to mine since Ashlee had come through the door. It was 9:08 a.m. and she was lucky because at

9

one minute past a quarter after, I would have been making her reschedule – juicy gossip or not. She had a fifteen minute grace period and that's it. We stuck to the script at MAD and didn't play tardiness with staff or customers.

Juke and Nel were going to have to pay the penalty *again* because they were late as usual. I wondered if Selena called off or would she also be paying the penalty since she hadn't walked in yet either. She's been getting here later and later herself. Me – I'd rather drag myself out of bed every morning, no matter how I'm feeling, instead of getting docked twenty-five dollars for the day just for being late. I can do a lot with that! It just makes more sense to me to just call off! Kenzie made an extra two-fifty a week off them two alone, sometimes two-seventy-five to three hundred, if one or both of them happened to have appointments scheduled on Mondays.

MaKenzie didn't stop there either– if you were going to be more than thirty minutes late, you may as well stay home. That was never a good thing because business was always booming at the shop. If someone had to cover a slot for you, not only did the customer pay the barber or stylist for the service, but you had to pay them as well - for the inconvenience. It was "All about the customers," Kenzie would say whenever someone would bitch about breaching the contract they signed. "We don't let money walk out the door. Don't make appointments that you are not going to keep. That's bad for business. It's only fair that you pay someone for doing *your* job." She had a point there, I thought.

Of course they both showed up in the nick of time, pushing it - Juke at 9:18 a.m. and Lanel strolled in at 9:29, with only seconds to spare. This close to being turned back around and sent out the door back to wherever they came from, yet still fifty more dollars in Kenzie's pocket because of the late fees.

The shop is what one would call upscale. The prices were upscale as well, but people didn't mind paying seeing as though they could enjoy other perks and bonuses while they waited. It was twenty-five dollars just to sit in the chair and that was on top of the price for the service you were there to receive. The guys played sports games on the PS3, shot a couple games on the free-play pool table, or lifted weights in the exercise room. All those things were located on the top floor.

When you first walked in, you were greeted by the barbers. Kenzie's office was in the middle of the shop through a door on the right. If you headed towards the back, you would find the women working their magic on their clients. Spin the bend, and there was a lounge area where the pool table and game consoles were. It even had a dart board and some arcade game where you shot at zombies. In the very back of the shop is where you would find the exercise room. Sometimes guys would pay just to come to the shop and lift weights – probably to try to hit on the ladies who would also be in there working out.

There was also a lower level to the shop which we called the MAD Underground Lounge. Paying customers received a complimentary drink and a shot (or soda or water for the non-alcoholics) and could enjoy free snacks and hors' devours. The drinks were served in the Underground and you could enjoy a game or movie while you waited. There were 55" flat-screens and a jukebox down there. If you weren't a customer waiting for a service, there was a fee to enter and a three drink maximum was in place for everyone – after all it wasn't an actual "bar". Clients are currently being served by their assigned stylist, or whoever isn't busy, while MaKenzie looks for a new bartender to run the Lounge. She fired the last broad for stealing money. Those cameras catch everything and ol' girl was putting the cash straight in her tip box instead of the register.

In the mornings there was assorted fruit danishes, fruit, orange juice and throughout the day you could enjoy your choice of bruschetta, assorted cheeses with crackers, and tea sandwiches – all of which the Dixons ordered and had delivered fresh daily. On occasion, Kenzie would grace us with her fire, homemade buffalo chicken dip or my favorite, her famous salmon dip. People also had the option of helping themselves to small, brown paper bags of popcorn or some pistachios from the machines located near the barbers at the front of the shop. I loved it here!

I was working my creative magic on Ashlee's nails. She was fresh out of high school and felt that being eighteen made her grown. She was a little wild for her age. She always had some gossip for me and today was no different.

"So, where's Selena?" she asked. "She probably still with Sledge. I saw them two at Eat N' Park this morning eating breakfast together."

I looked up when she said Sledge's name to see if Carmen was paying any attention. She wasn't. She would have had a fit if she'd heard what Ashlee said because she was just telling Bella he hadn't answered his phone for her since yesterday afternoon. I just know there is going to be some drama between them two soon.

I diverted the conversation, finished her up and got her out of there with the quickness before Carmen caught wind of her gossip. I cashed her out and went to MaKenzie's office.

"What's up Miss Lady, you booked all day I see."

I had checked up on her schedule before going in there. We each had phones mounted on the wall and monitors encased in glass right next to them at our stations. Those monitors showed each of our schedules by choosing the color-coded squares with our initials in them. It was touch screen and I had pushed the red to bring up Kenzie's schedule. I saw that her last appointment was at 11:30 p.m.

"Yeah, Reese is out of town until tomorrow, so I figured why not. How many you have for today miss?"

"My nine o'clock just left and I only have three more appointments scheduled. At 11:30, 2:00, and the last one is at 4:30," I told her.

"Oh okay. Nitra, can you do me a favor and close Greg's books in the system for this week? He took off for today."

"Yea, sure, I can do that. Do you need me to stay late with you tonight or is it ok if I close my books too for today, after my last appointment? My friend is going to a cookout at Schenley Park and I'd like to go with her."

She seemed to be in a good mood so I figured I would use it to my advantage. After all, Greg took the day off, and it looks like Selena did too and she wasn't tripping about that. That girl was starting to miss a lot and I knew MaKenzie was growing tired of it. I wouldn't be surprised if she is replaced by a new stylist soon the way she's been – which is very inconsistent lately. This place was a gold mine for success and especially on a day like today. Kenzie runs this shop like a true business woman. She wanted us to commit to "shifts" which meant being available for regular shop hours – working twelve hour days, six days a week and only one was by appointment only. Beyond normal working hours was by appointment only also and we found our twelve hour days turning into sixteen *easy*. It was a Saturday and the weekends were always the busiest. I might be pushing it today, but hell, she's not pressed for money, plus I was always on my job – did I say I love it here!

13

"Sure." She had a look that says she was counting up what I stood to make in her head, "Put your money in the books for today and close out. I'll give you your pay now," she obliged.

I had four appointments for today and each of my customers wanted a full set with French manicured tips. *Easy!* I busted out my next three clients, served drinks to customers, all while answering calls and setting appointments in between for the whole MAD Crew. I washed two heads for Carmen, swept up hair for Lanel who was cutting back-to-back with no break since he got here, and even sparred in a rip session with Juke's silly ass until I was done for the day.

Of course the shop just wouldn't be the shop without some true characters showing up at the spot and today was no different. Drunken ass Harry, whom we called "Two Times" came up in there talking bout he needed to make some money so he could buy himself a bottle of Taylor's Port. "At least he's honest," Bella said. Lanel gave him some play by letting him wash his car in the back lot. He had that silver Mercedes looking right once he was done too. He earned his bottle for sure. Nel gave him a nice tip and he stayed true to his name by doing his drunken ass dance that he always did 'two times' before staggering off. Four thirty was here before I knew it and I was happy to be done early for the day. Harry gave me just the laugh I needed to send me off with a smile.

"I'll holla! Have a good weekend My Mad Peoples!"

I was out of there until Monday.

14

Friends...

It was days like this I wished I had a car. It was beautiful outside. The sun was kissing my body and beads of sweat started to form on the tip of my nose as I made my way to the bus stop. I would love to be whipping around with the windows down, hair blowing in the wind with the music playing. I'd be singing along, belting tunes out from the pit of my stomach like I was a contestant on The Voice or something. It's all good though. I'm saving up and in due time, my thoughts will become my reality.

After a good ten minutes, I finally saw the bus approaching from down the street. At the same time, my attention was redirected by the sound of "There goes my baaabyyy" coming from somebody's car. That's my ringtone for Jax because he always plays that song when we're together. I was hoping he decided to drop in town to see me and a ride home would be a nice and welcomed surprise, but of course that wasn't the case. The music was coming from a black and red Ford F-150 sitting across the street at the light. It was sitting pretty and was clean as a whistle. The driver and I caught eyes and I felt an instant attraction. The man staring back at me was fine as hell. The bus pulled up and blocked our view of each other and I got on. I heard car horns beeping as I sat at a window seat, looking to see what was going on. He was still watching me. He smiled, I smiled back and he pulled off. I fantasized about him the whole ride home. I would love it if he were present at the cookout in the park later on. I was tickled by him holding up traffic and his smile was so infectious that I already wanted to see him again.

As usual my thoughts shifted to Jax. I wanted it to be him in that truck, playing that song, however I knew that was wishful thinking. I am growing tired of waiting. Waiting on him to feel a man's touch, waiting on him to get a window of time out of his hectic life to spend with me. Growing more and more wary as the days go by, knowing our situation is hopeless. He's done so much dirt that he can't live in the state and I have to settle for impromptu visits from him to get my groove on. He doesn't want me seeing anyone else but this thing we have just isn't enough for me anymore and hasn't been for a long time. I've already decided that we'd stay friends - with benefits *for now*, but to hell with trying to hold on to the wind. His lifestyle is dangerous and I'm too young to live in fear every day of my life. I don't know if he does what he does for the money or for fun but either way, it doesn't sit well with me. That's not what I want, nor what I deserve. I deserve a man who I can at least imagine getting old with. I see myself visiting him in some dirty ass jail, or worse, at a funeral home preparing to bury him by the time I'm twenty-five. He just has too much going on. I love him but I'm not in love with him, yet he's the only man I'm comfortable around. Perhaps because I know he can protect me, I guess. I have trust issues. But – to hell with all this… It's my stop and I'm off to get ready to enjoy my night.

~~~~~~~

Woke up the next morning with a headache, reminding me of the night I had. I live with my maternal grandmother, Lorene, and the smell of breakfast cooking had me floating in mid-air to the direction of the kitchen like they do in commercials.

The cookout at Schenley Park was off the chain. Everybody and their momma were in attendance. The problem with that is, where there's alcohol and egos, add some strong

16

personalities multiplied by drugs and gangster music – divided by those getting it and those wanting to get it – it was a mixture equal to some straight Drama. Rarely could people from all sides of town come together without some bullshit popping off, and even though we knew something was bound to happen, we still continued to show up to see just who was going to show out.

A couple of guys had beef with each other and started arguing about some shady shit that went down during a crap game near the playground. Next thing you know, there were herds of people running to their rides, trying not to catch a bullet that didn't belong to them. Fortunately, no one was hit – even though there had to be at least thirty shots fired. And that actually doubled as the sad part – aimless bullets flying around – missing intended targets, while putting innocent people in danger.

After eating breakfast, I headed to the bathroom to shower and brush my teeth. That meal hit the spot and had me feeling a little bit better, especially since the headache went from a nine to a three on the scale. I stopped in my room first to see what I was going to wear on this lovely day. I noticed the light on my cell flashing, indicating I had a missed call or a message. I picked it up off my dresser and saw it was a missed call from my neighbor Leslie who lived across the street.

Les was twenty-five years old with no children, living on her own, and did nothing but braid hair, smoke loud and gossip all day. She was a beast with her braiding skills and everybody and they grandmama went to her to get them done. She was never broke, even though she suffered from a repetitive stress injury from braiding day in and day out. I called her back and told her I'd be over after I got dressed. She wanted to tell me about her escapade with dude she brought home from the cookout last night. That girl is a mess I tell ya!

When I got to Leslie's house, it was about quarter to twelve and already she was on her grind. When I saw whose hair she was braiding, I just knew it was a set up. Jax was sitting in between her legs, puffing on some loud, getting a style like a biker from a page Les had ripped out of a magazine.

"You called me over here for him didn't you?"

"Nah, I was seeing if you wanted to blaze and tell you 'bout ole boy's stankin' ass last night."

Jax chimed in, "Don't act like you're not happy to see me. I know I'm happy to see you. Damn Bae, you looking good in them shorts. Come over here and give me some love."

He was right; I was happy as hell to see him. I was only stubborn towards him because I couldn't see him more. I couldn't *really* be mad at him because I understood why.

He was doing too much and stayed in some shit when he lived in Pittsburgh. His mother wasn't with it and sent him to Maryland to live with his uncle. That's where he's been for the last nine years. She was determined not to lose her son to the streets and shipped him out when he turned sixteen.

He *was* my boyfriend at the time that he left, but as I got older, the long distance thing became too much for me after a while. We, well I, decided we'd always be friends, and that came with some benefits whenever he came to town to visit – which was basically during the summertime and holidays at first. As he got older his trips to and from the Burgh started to increase. He slid in and out of town on occasion, coming back to handle business and to see me of course.

He stood up and passed the blunt to Les as I made my way over to him standing with his hair half done. I grabbed what was undone and pulled it, gently pulling his face close to mine. He held me tightly around my waist and I put my arms around his neck as we kissed – passionately.

"I…missed…you," I said placing kisses on his lips with each word. Leslie cleared her throat and told us to get a room.

He looked in her direction, "I already got that covered."

She sucked her teeth and shook her head from side to side, "Yall make such a cute couple. Too bad yall won't just quit playing and be together."

He turned back to me and looked me in my eyes, "We can if she would just move with me. I don't stay with my Unc anymore. I got my own place now." He grabbed up his keys and jingled them in my face. Holding them by the key that belonged to his place I guess.

"Jax, I can't just up and leave my grandma knowing she's sick. You know I couldn't do that. I have to be here to help her. Who else is going to take care of her? I keep telling you that."

"I know Bae. And it's only right you help take care of Ms. Lorene. I love yall's bond and the respect and care yall have for one another. Wishful thinking, I guess."

Leslie interrupted, "Come on… Let me finish your head. Yall can do all yall catching up in that room yall got for tonight. I got shit to do." He let go of my waist and took his position back on the floor.

She finished his hair at around two o'clock. He checked out the style she put on him in the mirror and tipped her twenty extra dollars. He then looked at me and told me to go pack an

19

overnight bag. He said to be ready for him to pick me up at eight so we could roll out. He didn't have to tell me twice.

Since Leslie and I never got around to what happened last night, I told her I'd come right back over to have that conversation after I packed my bag.

When I did go back over there, she was on the phone arguing with some broad. She held up her finger, signaling me to give her a second and continued to give the girl the business over the phone. When she hung up, she busted out laughing, "Simple bitches. Don't check me, check ya man. Fuck wrong with these ducks Nitra?"

I just shook my head, "Girl, You... you're what's wrong with them. You gon' mess around and have somebody at your doorstep ready to kick a bone out your ass about their man one day."

"Phaaa... And that's the day I'll have my first charge for murdering one of them bitches. That was dude's woman from last night. How he ended up here and not there is her problem, and her problem only. Don't call me with that crap. Shit – I don't want his ass no way. Girl, he took his shoes off so we could cuddle and watch a movie and stunk up the whole damn house. Unh unh... She can keep his funky ass."

I started laughing out loud at the face she had. It was as if she could still smell it. From the look on her face, the shit must have smelled foul.

She continued to tell me about how she kicked his ass out and told him to never come back. She has no filter so I'm sure he was mad as hell about the choice words that flew off her tongue. He won't be looking to cross paths with her anytime soon.

~~~~~~

Later that night, I was sitting on my porch, browsing on Facebook when Jax pulled up. I shut down my Kindle, placed it in my bag and headed to the car. I called the house phone to tell my grandma not to wait up and make sure she locked the door before she went to bed.

"I see Jayson's in town. Where yall headed?" she asked. She must have looked out the window when she heard his music as he pulled up in front. "Since when he come and....." She heard a knock at the door. "Hold on a minute."

She opened the door and Jax greeted her with a hug. "How are you Ms. Lorene? I was in town and wanted to pick Nitra up and take her out to eat or something. She's staying with me tonight. Is that alright?"

"Hey baby, I was just telling Nee Nee you better not be in front of the house and not come and say something to me. Give me some sugar pumpkin," she said, offering him her cheek. "I wish you two would make a way to be with each other. She's so happy when she's with you."

For the second time today, someone was telling him we needed to be an official couple. That's how close we were.

"I wish the same thing Ms. Lorene. She's not going to leave you though. You know how much she cares about you and your health Ms. Lorene." He looked back at me and then back to her, "But I'll wait. All she has to do is say the word and I'll come running. She knows that."

My grandma smiled and started patting him on the shoulder, "You sure are a good young man with a good heart.

21

You know that? What's meant to be will be. You two enjoy yourselves. I'm taking these old bones to bed."

I yelled, "See you tomorrow Grandma."

Jax said his goodbyes, "Thanks and Okay Ms. Lorene. Take care."

"Take care Jayson – and take care of my baby."

"No Doubt!"

...And Lovers

We went to Yokoso – The Japanese Steakhouse in the Waterfront for dinner. We sat at the bar and had a couple drinks while we waited to be seated. Jax got to telling me about his new spot down Maryland and how he wanted me to come and visit sometime soon, saying it could use a woman's touch.

"When?" I asked him with an arched brow, "I have some appointments scheduled for tomorrow. I'm actually booked all week, but I promise I'll come down soon."

"Oh yeah, how's that coming? You still working at that upscale joint, MAD Styles or something like that right?"

"Yea, that's it. It's cool. Business is good and I like the atmosphere. Not to mention the Dixon's got it laid out up in there. You need to come through one day and check it out. I've only been there over a year now and you haven't been there once."

"Maybe I'll come get a shape-up or something."

"Yea, and my boss, MaKenzie – she does it all. Come let her give you a massage or facial or something. You'll love it. Plus you'll receive a complimentary drink and shot while you're there."

"Word! They doing it like that?"

"Man, just come through. You'll love the place, I'm telling you."

"I'll be through, but you sure you want ol' girl to be rubbing all over this," he said, playfully rubbing his hands over his chest.

I punched him playfully in the arm, "MaKenzie is happily married. She's bout that cash, so Yea, I'm cool with it."

We were called to our table shortly after I finished my second drink. We were seated with three other couples.

"Well speak of the devil." I couldn't believe my eyes when I recognized we were sitting with Reese, MaKenzie's husband, and he was with some woman who was not her. I'm thinking, surely she had to be family or something. There's no way he'd bring another woman on a date so close to the home he shared with his wife. He noticed me staring and gave me a head nod. I returned the nod and quickly looked back down at my menu. I started thinking - this little encounter could be my job on the line and decided to just mind my business. People tend to always want to kill the messenger anyway. I'm not married to him and he doesn't owe me any explanation, so as far as I'm concerned – it has nothing to do with me and I'm staying out of it. I chalked it up as him, perhaps, being with family since this would be along the lines of "shitting where you eat" and I hoped Reese was smarter than that.

I couldn't help but pay a little attention to how they interacted with each other, but from what I could see, they were just enjoying a good meal and conversation. Where's the harm in that? – Shoulder shrug! There was no touchy-feely shit going on so maybe this meeting between the two was innocent... *or business maybe?* – I don't know! But I'll tell you what; I will not be the one to start some shit based on speculation. As far as I knew, MaKenzie and Reese were happy together and he made sure to keep a smile on her face, making sure she had everything she needed and giving her any and everything she wanted, so who was I to question him.

I turned my attention back to Jax who wasn't slow to anything. He had noticed me staring and the head nods, but waited until after dinner to ask me about it. I knew for sure he had some questions, especially since Reese paid our bill. Jax wasn't broke in the least and I could tell he wasn't feeling that.

"What the fuck was that all about? I know that ain't no nigga you fuckin' wit'?"

"What?" I asked, playing stupid for no reason.

"I saw the head nods between you and the cat with the dreads – not to mention dude just paid our bill as if I needed his fucking help or some shit."

"Oh! That was my boss' husband, the one we were just talking about. At first I got to thinking maybe he needed *our help* to keep this little encounter on the low, wondering who he was with, but then I got to thinking I better mind my business. Reese's money is long. I'm sure he didn't think you needed his help – he probably was just being nice to his wife's employee", I reasoned.

Then I continued on, "He can't be that stupid to be cheating so close to home. I mean, doesn't he know he's bound to be seen, flaunting his mistress in public. Let me stop. I don't know anything about them. Again, I'm just going to mind my damn business."

Jax knew better. He was a playa himself and knew the game when he saw it being played. That broad was definitely not any kin to that man. He wasn't about to throw another man under the bus so he changed the subject, "What you wanna do next?"

We decided to go to Dave & Busters and play a few games before we ended our night at the Comfort Inn Suites.

~~~~~~~~

We got to the room about twelve-thirty. It was just like being in our own apartment. It had an upstairs and downstairs, two bathrooms – one on each level, a kitchen complete with a stove and refrigerator, and a cozy living room area.

"What the hell you need all this space for?" I asked him, looking around at the spacious surroundings.

"I don't like staying in them little boxes you call a room. I need to feel at home wherever I lay my head. I'll be here for five days or so. Got some things to handle, so this is like my home away from home for the time being. Feel me? Even more-so now that you're here with me."

He took a seat on the sofa and patted his hands on his lap gesturing for me to come take a seat. I sat down on his lap, straddling him and put my arms around his neck as we engaged in our second passionate kiss of the day. It was a warm, wet, tongue-filled kiss that was good enough to cause some moisture down below – which it had. His manhood started to bulge, poking at that place, making me want to skip all foreplay and get right to it. I ran my hands up his chest and took his shirt off, slowly and in one motion, not wanting to waste any more time – running them back down his chest until I reached his belt. Our lips were still locked in a warm embrace. I unbuckled it and then unbuttoned his pants to give me better access to his member as he lifted my shirt over my head, displacing my arms for a moment. He stepped out of his shorts as I stepped out of mine

26

and time stopped for a minute as we stared at each other, admiring our views collectively. He grabbed a handful of the back of my hair and started kissing me again. I was turned on by his aggression.

Instead of going upstairs to the master bedroom, he went to another room opposite the living area and pressed a button on the wall. A bed began lowering to the floor. I turned around and he unhooked my bra in one swoop with his free hand and it was on from there.

He smacked it, He flipped it
He even rubbed me down
He took me fast, He took me slow
In and out and Round and Round

Heavy breathing and Sexy sex faces
Different positions... Sweaty embraces
Making love in the bed, in the shower, on the floor
And all kind of places...

I rode him in a chair.
He bent me over with my hands on the wall,
While I screamed, "Ooooh yea Baby, Right There!"

He laid me down, legs propped on his shoulders...

Entering deeper and deeper
Speeding up, then pacing ourselves
As our bodies grew weaker and weaker

SPLASH! – Our waves crashed...

Striking nerves, causing limbs to spasm
I squirt and I jerk from the skill of his work
As we both collapsed from explosive orgasms.

Cue the mutha-fuckin fire works!!....

"Damn Jax, that was some good shit, as always." He didn't respond. *I did my thing as usual*! I took up residence in between his legs with my back against his chest. The television was on but we were more in to each other.

"Jax, you know one day this will have to end right?"

"What, Us? Nah, why you say that? I keep telling you you're mine forever. You think I be playing when I say that?"

I giggled a little, "Yeah, I'm your *friend* forever, but if I get into something serious with someone else, the benefits are going to have to stop. Ain't no man going to be with all that 'Oh, that's my best friend' shit."

"Where is all this coming from", he asked as he sat up straighter, making me lift up off him. "You seeing somebody or something?" He had a slight scowl on his face as I turned to look at him. He looked serious, but I saw love in his eyes.

"Not yet, but I think I'm ready to. What about you? You find a girlfriend in Maryland yet?"

"I have a friend, that's a girl. Nothing serious, just someone I'm talking to right now." The skin between his brows softened when he spoke of her.

"Is she pretty?"

"Yea, she's pretty. She kind of look like you."

"Well, she might look like me but, She (peck)....Ain't (peck)....Me (peck)," placing kisses on his lips as I said the last three words.

"She sure ain't. That's why you need to come live with me. I....Want....You," he said, pecking at my lips the same way I did him.

"Come on Jax. That's our issue right there. You know I'm not leaving my grandma and you're not moving back to Pittsburgh, so stop saying that please. The long distance thing would certainly not work out for me. You already know that. I don't trust your sexy ass in another state where I can't keep my eyes on you."

We cuddled for the rest of the night, both lost in our own thoughts. Me, knowing we were going to have to stop meeting like this eventually – and him, holding on to hope that I would change my mind and go away with him one of these days. *Not gonna happen, Captain*!

He says it's nothing serious between him and this "girl that's a friend", but I know better. He has always denied seeing anyone, until now. Even if he was, he wouldn't acknowledge them to me because he wanted me to feel like I was the only one that mattered. The fact that he admitted to talking to her meant he was feeling her. It may not be serious, yet, but she has surely captured his attention - enough for him to acknowledge her when I asked if he had a girlfriend. And now that I knew she was there, Jax and I can be friends, but I want my own man.

June 13th... We Meet Again

The next morning, I hit the shower as soon as I woke up. He wanted to get in with me like he usually did but I refused. If he got in with me, we'd end up having sex again and since I had to be to work in an hour, "We better not". The truth was I decided to start weaning myself from him before I got my feelings hurt. There was no way to get around hurting his.

He called in an order for pick-up, knowing I'd enjoy some breakfast from Pamela's before going in to work. We picked up the food and he took me to the shop, neither of us saying a word the whole ride.

MaKenzie was already there when I got there and as usual, I was the first worker on the clock. Reese's truck, plus another, was outside and her office door was shut, so I didn't bother knocking for fear I'd be interrupting something. I'm sure they knew I was there anyway since the camera monitors were in there with them. I figured there was no need to disturb them. The other truck outside looked identical to the one I saw at the light a couple days ago, but I'm thinking it has to be a coincidence. What would he be doing here?

I checked the schedules from my station as I sat down to eat my breakfast. Jax called my cell phone. Although it was in my purse, I knew it was him from the ringtone. I made a mental note to change that. I shuffled around the bottom of my purse until I located my phone, but by then I'd missed his call. "There goes my baaaaby" came singing through again. This time I pushed the end button.

He knows me like the back of his hand so I'm sure he knew what was going on in my head. I didn't have to say a word. My actions spoke volumes – I ALWAYS answered his calls – no matter what. *Not this time Buddy*!

I received a text notification: *Don't be like that... I want to spend another night with you so we can TALK. What time you getting off?*

After not receiving a response from me, he texted again: *I'll be outside when you get off. Be there around 7:45.*

I had already told him last night that I was working eight to eight today so I don't know why he asked a question he already knew the answer to in the first place.

Dammit! I'll just try and finish up early and leave at 7:15. We can't keep doing this – I can't keep doing this.

The door to MaKenzie's office whisked open and she, her husband, and another gentleman emerged from behind the doors. The fine specimen of a man and I locked eyes for a brief moment as MaKenzie turned and greeted me, "Hey Nitra, first one here as usual," she said with a smile.

"Hey Kenzie... Hey Reese," I smiled back at the both of them. Oh, and *him* too. *It was him – the guy from the other day – I can't believe it!* Reese gave me that same head nod he gave me last night at Yokoso's.

"Nitra, this is Haji, Greg's friend. He will be taking over the cleaning contract."

"Oh, okay. Hi Haji, I'm Anitra. Nice to meet you," I said, walking in their direction, extending my hand for a handshake.

He raised it and kissed it instead. "Nice to meet you too," he said, prolonging his hold on my hand.

"There goes my baaaaby" came playing through my phone *Again*. He released my hand as I went back to my station, this time wanting to curse Jax's ass out for ruining my moment.

"YES" I answered sternly.

"7:45" he said.

"Yea, okay, now Bye. I have work to do."

"See you soon" – Click!

I looked at my phone and shook my head – "He is not going to let me be," I thought to myself. Reese came over and pulled me to the side and asked if I could close tonight so he could take MaKenzie out somewhere for some QT. He said he wasn't feeling comfortable enough to give dude a key just yet. He told me Haji would be starting tonight and he needed me to do that favor for them.

"Um, okay. What time you need me to stay until?"

"Well, he's supposed to come back at eight. Since the last appointment scheduled is yours, I thought we'd ask you to close. Cool?"

"Yeah that's cool."

They all left the shop, leaving me with my thoughts, thinking about how I'm going to get out of staying with Jax tonight. I was kind of happy they asked me to stay late.

I received another text notification: Check your drawer was all it said. The number wasn't stored as a contact in my phone, so I'm wondering *What the hell?* I opened my drawer and apparently there was five hundred in hush money sitting there with a note I assumed was from Reese that simply read: Thank You! – with a smiley face. *Hmmm!* Now this is odd. I wasn't sure if he was thanking me for staying late while he played kiss-up with Kenzie, or thanking me for not running my mouth and ruining his marriage. Either way, I appreciated the bonus, and since I'm uncertain of his relationship with that woman last night, I don't plan on saying anything anyway. *"Nuccas got some shit with them"*, I thought.

It was business as usual and everyone had appointments except Juke. It was Monday – which was an appointment only day and he made sure he extended his weekend by not putting anyone on his schedule. He was spoiled by his aunt and her husband of nine years, and he didn't want for anything. Missing a day was nothing to him. He was going to eat either way. Sadly, even though that was the case, he couldn't get enough and was into things he had no business – and somehow managed to do the shit without it being detected by his guardians – or so I thought. He wasn't necessarily a little boy, but Juke was definitely not ready to care for himself, or be a responsible adult for that matter – which is why he still lived in their basement.

I considered Selena, one of the stylists, to be laid back – pretty much stayed to herself. Whenever she did open her mouth though, she always had something slick to say. She was a Sanaa

Lathan look-alike, with a Lisa Raye body and a smart ass mouth. I hope she packs a Laila Ali punch because that mouth of hers is going to get her into some trouble one of these days. She was in-between clients and her phone started singing, "I can love you better than she can." She was on her Bluetooth in her own little world, talking to someone while she touched up her hair in the mirror.

I ear hustled on her conversation while doing my client's nails…

"Hey you! How'd you steal away some time to call me?" She asked the caller. She let out a little giggle and continued, "Aw, don't I feel special… Nah, its cool, I understand… Mmmhm, I hear you…You crazy baby, but that's why I love you." She listened for a bit as she sat down and twirled the ends of her jet black, curly hair with her index finger, biting on her bottom lip with a smile. "Okay Baby, I'd love that. Don't have too much fun – you know I'm jealous… See you tomorrow." The caller said something else and she said, "Okay, okay… Bye Baby."

Carmen must have been ear hustling too. She was on her shit today, as usual. "I know you wasn't talking to my man," she said with her hand on her hip.

Selena replied, "If that was your man on my phone, then I guess he won't be tomorrow." Several of us busted out in laughter.

"Whatever," was all Carmen said as she continued working on her client's hair. "He don't want your ass no way, I was just fucking with you."

Selena's next client walked in the door and it was back to business. The showdown is coming soon – I can feel it.

We closed up shop around a quarter after seven, with Selena being the last to leave for a change. If you asked me, she only liked being here when MaKenzie wasn't. *I wonder what that's all about?* I'm going to ask MaKenzie what's up with her. She might as well quit. She has no good business ethics – never here and when she is, she's late and then has the nerve to leave early half the time. Like I always say, "Must be Nice."

The day was over so I decided to tidy my station while I waited for Haji to return. It's crazy we crossed paths two days ago and now we meet again – and he'll be working here with his sexy self. I'm sure I will never get enough of seeing him. Gotta love a hard-working man, looking good in his work clothes. Shit, he could work me, I mean for me, any day.

Trouble Brewing

Jax pulled up at 7:45 as promised. I told him to come in for a minute. His sexy ass walked through that door and almost made me forget the real reason I called him in there, but I had to stick to the script. I told him I couldn't leave with him because Kenzie and Reese asked me to lock up. I set the buzz-entry system since we were officially closed for the day. *Don't need any crazies bringing there asses up in here. They don't understand* "CLOSED" *– even though it's displayed in the window in bright red letters.*

"I'll wait while you do that."

"No. Someone new took over the cleaning contract and they're starting tonight. They still feeling him out until they feel they can trust him enough to give him a key. He's new, so I'm sure it's going to take him a while until he gets used to the routine."

I didn't want or need him around knowing I had an attraction to the guy.

"Him?" he said, raising his left eyebrow. "The fool whose truck was outside this morning when I dropped you off huh? I'm not slow to nothing Nee. Don't' try to play me."

"Come on Jax. Even if he was here for me, which he wasn't, you and I are just friends anyway. Plus you're seeing someone remember? Don't be trying to cock-block. That term works both ways ya know," I laughed. He didn't crack a smile.

36

"Don't play with me Nee."

"Ain't nobody playing. Well except for the cock blocking part, but you *do* have a girlfriend and she is not me, right?"

"You would be if you stop fucking playing and come be with me. I told you it isn't serious with ol' girl."

"*Yet!*" I said, "But she was serious enough for you to acknowledge her *so*… same thing."

"Man…She's just something to do. What? Am I supposed to beat my dick when I'm not in Pittsburgh? I can't be assaulting my mans like that. Until you ready to come be with me, I gotta do *something*."

"Nah Bruh, you want your cake and you want to eat it too… typical."

"Well what's the point of having cake if you can't eat it too," he joked. This time I was the one who wasn't laughing.

"Ha-ha-ha… Nah, yo ass want 'hoes in different area codes'. Well, the buck stops here with me. I'm serious Jax. Friends – No Benefits – Friends," I reiterated, pointing my pretty manicured finger in his face.

Haji rang the buzzer, startling both of us, halting our conversation. I was 'saved by the bell', seeing the frustration that was written all over Jax's face. I pressed the button to release the lock, letting him in.

"Hey Nitra. I got here as soon as I can. I tried to make it earlier since they said the last appointment was at seven tonight, but something came up."

"It's cool. You're still ten minutes early by my watch. I wasn't expecting you until eight anyway. It's all good. Greg usually starts from the Lounge and works his way up." I said, pointing the way towards the elevator.

"Yeah, Reese and his wife put me on to the routine and gave me a tour of the place before you got here this morning."

Mmmmm...There was something about his bedroom eyes... and his chest - Yes! He was wearing a white wife beater, looking good enough to eat. He stood a little taller than me – probably about five-foot-eleven I'm guessing. I'm five-foot-eight and he wasn't towering that much over me so I think that's a fair guess.

"Oh, okay," I said, still staring at his handsome self standing before me. "Well I'll be right here when you're done."

"Okay cool," he responded as he pushed his sweeper towards the back, taking the elevator down to the underground, not even so much as acknowledging Jax sitting there. Although I felt the heat rise up in here as they caught eyes when Haji first walked in, I chopped it up to my hoe down below, excited about having not one, but two handsome mandingos in the same space at the same time. *"No ma'am, Don't even think about it!"* I shot her ass down.

Jax spoke up, jarring me from my thoughts, "Oh, so no introduction? You staring and shit? Don't disrespect me in my face like that ever again. I'll fuck you and that nigga up."

"What? What did you just say?"

That was the first time he'd ever threatened to harm me and playing or not - it was also going to be his last.

"You know what? ... Thank You! You just made things that much easier for me... Bye Jax. Go on back to Maryland and talk that shit to your girlfriend. I can do what the fuck I want," I said, opening the door for him to leave.

"Come on Nee…"

"BYE Jax."

"I can't believe you're acting like this. Man, I'll call you. Answer your phone or I'll be at your fucking door."

He got in his car and burned a little rubber before pulling off. "*Corny*," I thought, as I watched him speed off in a tantrum until he turned the bend at the corner.

Haji emerged from the lounge about a half an hour later. No one had used the exercise or game rooms today, so he didn't need to do anything in there tonight. We made small talk as he swept, mopped and buffed the marble floors.

"So how long you been working here?"

"Almost a year and a half now."

"This spot kinda nice. When they showed me around earlier I was impressed with the layout."

"Yea, it is nice. I plan to open my own nail shop one day. I have some ideas of my own and I won't stop until I make them my reality. I've drawn a lot of inspiration from MaKenzie. She's a really cool person."

"Oh yea, that's wassup. A lot of young ladies aren't thinking about doing anything with themselves now days so that's refreshing to hear. A young woman with dreams and aspirations - that goes beyond looking for a handout or a sugar daddy to take care of her. What they call it - a sponsor?"

We both laughed. There is just something about him that makes me comfortable. I was totally fine being alone with this perfect stranger.

"Yea, that's what they call it. And no thank you – I can and will get it on my own. Kenzie is so sweet that she's teaching me everything she knows. I've shared my plans with her and she is determined to help me get there. I spend a lot of time in her office talking with her and assisting her with her clients when I'm not doing nails for my own. I plan on enrolling at Empire Beauty School to get my license. I've just been in no rush since it's going to take some time to raise the capital I need to get things started, but… I'm working on it. And I will be happy to say I did it all on my own – *without* the help of a sponsor."

We both laughed again.

"That's wassup. It's good you have a plan and you will succeed as long as you prepare and stay focused. You have to really want it - be passionate about it and make it happen. "

"I am. I really am. And I'm gonna make it happen. Don't believe me just watch!" I said that last part just like the song.

"Oh, I believe you. You just be sure to believe in yourself – Always."

We talked some more until he was done and I was actually amazed at how uninhibited I felt sharing some of my innermost thoughts and plans for my life with him. He was so easy to talk to. A great listener who also gave me some good business advice.

The gold specks on the black, tiled, marble flooring sparkled like it had just been laid. He cleaned the mirrors, emptied the trash and took it out back to the huge dumpsters that were out there. Since Kenzie was out on the town with her husband all day, he didn't need to touch her office either. A three hour job had been cut in half since he got a break on his first night – having three less areas to clean.

"How are you getting home, you drive?" he inquired. "Or your man coming back to get you?"

"The bus. I'm saving up for a car. And that wasn't my man." I wanted to make that clear.

"Oh okay. My bad. I can give you a ride if you need. I've got nothing else to do."

"Um, sure. Thanks!"

"My Pleasure."

In the fifteen minutes it took him to take me home in his F-150, it was obvious we were feeling each other - the enthrallment between us was evident and the chemistry was present from the start. Apparently he was doing a run-by past the shop the day I saw him at the light. He was checking the location of the spot before his meeting with Reese and MaKenzie. He said he was upset he didn't get a chance to say anything to me at that moment, but he was confident he would see me again. He planned to accept the contract just to increase his chances since that's where he first saw me. I laughed when he told me he was tempted to follow the bus until I got off but didn't want me to think he was some kind of stalker.

What he didn't know is I was feeling the same way, unable to stop thinking about him since I saw him. We both agreed that the odds were in our favor as we meet again - so soon.

"It must be meant to be. Don't you think?" He changed the course of the conversation.

I gave him the sexy side-eye, "What must be meant to be?

"You…Me…Us… Seeing each other and then working at the same place days later. You are so fine ma and just from talking to you I can tell I want you…I wasn't going to stop searching for you. I would have circled that block everyday hoping to see you again. But here you are… Mmm. I'm a lucky guy."

I giggled a little, "What makes you so lucky? There's nothing special about me."

"Oh but there is. I can see it. In your eyes, in your voice… your words… Your vibe is something special babygirl. A breath of fresh air…"

"Awe… how sweet. Well, thanks… although I don't see it."

Of course he asked about Jax again and I told him he was a friend who wanted more than I wanted out of the friendship.

"So, he's my competition then?"

"No competition. We are just friends."

"Does he get the benefits?"

I laughed and answered truthfully, "He has. That's probably why he's trippin'."

He smiled a sly smile, "I can't wait for the day you put it on me like that."

Well, aren't we mighty direct, I thought. *Only out for one thing I see. What a turn-off*! I looked at him like he'd just stunk up the truck after passing gas and said, "I see…"

He cut me off and cleaned it up real quick, "Even if it takes a whole year. I'll wait… but in the meantime, I want to finish getting to know you better."

"*He better had*," I thought as we pulled up in front of my house.

"See you tomorrow," he said with a grin.

"Yes, see you tomorrow. And thanks for the ride. I plan on getting me some wheels soon. Thanks again Haji."

I sincerely appreciated the ride home. It cut an hour ride on the bus down to fifteen minutes and I was grateful. This chick is tired.

"No problem. I enjoyed talking to you. You have a good head on your shoulders. And you're Beautiful... "

"Thanks, see you tomorrow," I repeated. I was blushing.

All We'll Ever Be

When I got in the house, my grandmother was already in her room ready for bed. I heard her coughing and it didn't sound good at all. I went up the steps, knocked once and entered since her door was cracked open.

She turned from her side and stated the obvious, "Hey Baby, you're home."

"Hey Grandma, yes, I'm home. How are you feeling? You sound like you need some water."

"A lil weak, but I'm alright. I have some water on my nightstand."

"Did you eat?" I asked as I picked up the pitcher of water, filling up her glass and inserting a new straw.

"Thank you. And yes, Jayson stopped by here a couple hours ago. Joyce made some liver and rice with gravy and he brought me a plate. Boy his mama sure can make some liver. He remembered…(cough, cough, sip) how much I enjoyed it the last time she sent me a plate, so he said he thought he'd bring me some since he knows I like it. I really like that boy you know… He told me he made a mistake and made a small threat because he was jealous of some guy who was around but… (cough, cough, cough, sip sip) …but he didn't mean it and you took him serious."

"Grandma, let's not talk about Jax. You can't even talk without sounding like you're coughing up a lung. He's darn right I took him serious. I don't take any type of threat lightly, especially when you're threatening to do bodily harm."

"He wouldn't hurt you Sweetness. Well, not physically I don't believe. I'd be surprised if he'd ever do such a thing. He loves you."

"Oh, so I guess he didn't tell you about his little girlfriend in Maryland now did he?"

"No, he didn't. But he *wants* you. That boy is in love with you. Anyone can see that and I have cataracts."

"Grandma, Jax isn't for me like that. We are good friends and that's all we'll ever be. You don't know him like I do. We can't be together..."

I kissed her on her cheek and stood to go to my room.

"Well, he asked me to talk to you and I told him I'd try. Find it in your heart to forgive him baby. Those were just words. Oh, and Nita was by here today."

"Oh yeah? Glad I locked the door to my bedroom. She always taking my stuff. What she want anyway?"

"She was just stopping by. Said she'd come back later in the week so she can see you. Said she wanted to talk to you about something. You know, I don't understand your mother. I don't know if she coming or going half the time. I wish she get herself together. Runn – (cough, cough, cough) – running around here chasing all these men. (cough cough)"

"I know... and Okay. Get some rest Gram. I'll be in my room if you need me."

I took my clothes off and slipped into an oversized tee-shirt with a picture of some lips dripping red lipstick – wearing nothing else underneath. I put a movie in and hit the switch to turn on the air conditioner. The night air was still humid and it

46

was almost midnight. I thought I heard a knock at the door, so I turned the television down. Sure enough there was another knock, this time faster and a little harder.

"Who is it" I yelled from the top of the steps, thinking it was probably my mother returning to say what she wanted to say to me earlier.

He and my grandmother said in unison, "It's Jax."

"Jax?!...How you know?" I asked my gram. "And since when you start calling him by his street name?" She got me tripping right now.

"I heard his music pull up."

"You heard his music pull up?" I had to laugh, "That could have been anybody's music grandma."

I went back to my room, slipped on my house shoes, took my robe from the hook on the back of my door and threw it on, making my way downstairs to see what he wanted. I really wasn't in the mood for his shit at the moment.

"Can I talk to you?" he said. As he looked up, I could see something was wrong from the look in his eyes. My heart softened up.

"Come on in. What's up? Why you look so down? Did something happen?"

He sat down on the couch and folded his hands, placing his forearms on his knees, looking down at the floor. He never looked up as he said, "I just got word that my lil cousin was shot." He spoke through clenched teeth, holding back tears.

"Oh my God! Which one?" I asked.

47

"Terrence… My Uncle Barry's son. He just called me."

"Oh my! He's only like sixteen, isn't he? Is he okay? Where was he hit? He's still alive right?" I started bombarding him with questions.

"Yea… sixteen. He was hit in his side. He's in surgery right now. I'm about to get on the road. I need to go back now instead of later this week like I originally planned. I need you Nee. I need your support. Come with me… Please? It doesn't sound good man…"

Tears were now creeping down both sides of his face as I heard my grandma sounding like she was coughing up her second lung. I told him to come upstairs with me so I could check on her.

When I went in my room after making sure she was okay, Jax was laying on my bed on his back with his hands behind his head, staring at the ceiling with tears still in his eyes. I closed my door and straddled myself on top of him, leaning forward and putting my hands in his.

"Baby. My gram is so sick right now. I'm afraid to leave her." I said in the softest voice possible, taking one hand and wiping tears from his face and kissing him on the lips.

"Yea, that cough didn't sound too good… I understand… but at least tell me you're not really done with me. I don't want to leave you on a sour note. Kiss me again. Your kisses taste so sweet."

I kissed him again, "We cool."

I was still done, but I didn't want to hurt his feelings at a time like this. He was hurting and I didn't want to hurt him any further if I didn't have to. I'm sorry, but friends is all we'll ever be from here on out.

"Oh and Thanks for bringing my gram a plate. She loves your mom's cooking," I said, trying to change the subject.

"You don't have to thank me. I love Ms. Lorene too. I would have brought you some but I know you don't like liver. Why you tryna change the subject?" He knows me so well, I thought to myself.

I kissed his neck and then his lips, biting on the bottom one and one thing lead to another. We had sex again. I felt it was a good way to send him off – my goodbye fuck – only he wasn't aware that I planned for this to be the last time it happens.

He was the only man to ever see my bedroom, let alone have sex in my bed. He was also the first person I *willingly* slept with and have been sleeping with ever since. I was thirteen and him fifteen when it first happened. If it weren't for the shit I went through, he would have been the one to take my virginity. Unfortunately, I was raped at the age of nine, but I don't want to revisit that right now. That was probably the reason I had no reluctance to give him some at such an early age. I already knew what to expect, only I *wanted* it with him.

I had a couple of guys over as company every now and then, but they weren't getting any action, except from "The Matrix" or something that was playing on the TV. I'm the type to get turned off real quick, so nothing ever came out of any of it. They usually ended up saying something stupid and I'd cut them off.

"Damn, you know I hate to hit and run, but I need to hit the road. I'd rather hold you all night but I have to go and check

49

on my peoples. I'll call you okay," he said as he pulled up his pants and started adjusting his Louis V. belt.

I got up and put my silk robe over my now naked body. He had pulled my shirt over my head when I was done riding him. He had flipped me over, wanting to suck on my breasts without anything obstructing his view of my body. I kissed his lips and told him he gets a pass considering the circumstances. I made him promise to call me when he got there so I know he made it alright and walked him to the door. He called me five hours later, letting me know he made it and that his cousin had also made it through surgery but was going to have a long recovery.

Makenzie: A woman With a Plan

The next day it was back to business once I returned to MAD Styles. I picked out a special outfit for the day since I now had someone I was trying to impress. I also volunteered to lock up so I could spend some time with Haji again. I wasn't giving anyone else a chance to try and step on my toes. I enjoyed talking with him and was definitely trying to get to know him better too. He might be just the man I was looking for – since I knew I couldn't be with Jax – for my own personal reasons.

Haji is twenty-six, runs his own business, fine as hell and interested in me, and hopefully I'd find out soon if he was working with something I could handle. I was intrigued by him for some reason and wanted to see what he's all about.

I got some pistachios from the machine and went to knock on MaKenzie's office door. I liked her a lot and I could tell she adored me by the things she shared with me and how she treated me.

"Come on in," she answered. "Hey Nitra, what's up?"

"Oh nothing. How was your date with the hubby last night?"

"Oh, it was nice. We went to eat and to see a movie is all – besides our steamy nightcap." She smiled, "How'd it go with Haji last night?"

I smiled at the mention of his name, "It went well. He got them floors shining doesn't he?"

"Girl, Yes! I almost took my shoes off coming in this morning, afraid to scratch them up with my heels," she said, laughing. "I saw the way he was checking for you – all eyeballing you up and down. Did he come on to you? Those floors aren't the only thing shining. So is that smile plastered on your face young lady."

I blushed harder, "Not really. He offered me a ride home. I accepted and we talked a little but nothing too serious happened. He seems like cool people though. Sexy too, I might add," I said with a wink, "Shoo – I was ready to come on *to him*."

She laughed at me. "He is a cutie. Especially that patch of white hair on the top of his head."

"He said it's his birthmark."

"I thought so. Thanks for volunteering to close tonight. I see what you up to… You're not fooling anybody… But uh, babygirl, my next appointment is due any minute – Can you do me a favor and print out a schedule on everybody for the week for me. Individually, not the collective view please?"

She was looking down at her watch, sounding like she was rushing me out of there.

"Okay, sure. I'll send it to the printer in your office."

"Okay, Good, Thanks."

She stood there in deep thought, biting her bottom lip. MaKenzie was going through something internally, but wasn't letting on to anyone, not even me but whatever it is, she seems to be handling it well. What I didn't know was that she was indeed dealing with some major issues and had plans to handle things her way. In the end – everyone would know. There was a time and place for everything and the perfectionist she is – she was going to wait until the timing was just right.

MaKenzie's next "appointment" looked kind of weird and didn't seem like he was there to receive any of the services she had to offer – unless she was doing or into something we didn't know about. He was a short, stalky white man with a bald head and scruffy facial hair, dressed in a brown tailored suit that made me feel like we'd time traveled back to the seventies and he was carrying a black briefcase.

He cleared his throat, "Uh, Good Afternoon. I'm here to see an uh, uh - MaKenzie Dixon."

Kenzie emerged from her office with the quickness and greeted him with a handshake.

"Hi, I'm MaKenzie. Right this way. Follow me," she said, pointing in the direction of her office.

All eyes were on them but she didn't seem to care. They both had tunnel vision and were focused on completing whatever business he was there for. As soon as Kenzie's door closed, Selena said, barely audible, yet we all still heard her, "I wonder what that's all about."

Carmen chimed in, "None of your damn business."

"Wasn't nobody talking to you." Selena retorted back. "Not today... Not with the bullshit today."

"And just what the fuck you gonna do, cause I'm definitely with the bullshit – on any day? Your simple ass so worried bout what MaKenzie doing when your ass is hardly ever here. She run this shit so she can do what she want to up in here."

"Oh, so who the fuck are you – MaKenzie's spokesperson now or some shit? Fuck outta here. Follow your own advice and mind your damn business."

53

Greg spoke up, "Come on yall, don't start. We have customers in here. Keep it professional."

Carmen rolled her eyes while Selena sucked her teeth simultaneously. Twenty minutes later Selena was finished with her client and announced she was done for the day.

"Must be nice," Bella said, "You stay cutting out early."

"Well, I work because I want to, not because I have to. My man has enough money to take care of the both of us, and some," Selena said, looking around as if she owned the world or some shit. She had a look of entitlement as she said it.

"Oh, well excuse me heffa... Don't take you and Carmen's drama out on me. I'm just saying. But go on Boo... Bet I won't say shit else to your ass since you wanna be smart all the damn time. I don't have shit to do with yall beef." Bella said.

"And who's your so-called man?" Carmen interjected as she twisted the marcel iron on the ends of her client's hair that was getting a doubie. "I hope you're not still trying to claim mine." She added a *Simple Bitch* at the end of that, under her breath – I heard her.

"None of your damn business – remember that? Get you some and stay out of mine Bitch – are you hard of hearing?" Selena barked as she cashed out her client and gathered up her belongings.

She couldn't get out of there fast enough. If she didn't – the Royal Rumble would be going down in a matter of minutes. I could see it on both their faces. I guess Selena decided to take the high road and opted not to entertain the conversation any longer. She logged out her account in the system and rolled out the door without saying another word to anyone.

As soon as Selena hit the door, Carmen grabbed up her phone, more than likely suspecting she was going to meet up with Sledge. It's really not a good look on her but she doesn't care. I personally thought she was too pretty to be so insecure. I mean, she wasn't anybody's runway model, but she was pretty in a Serena Williams kind of way. That's her celebrity look-alike (kinda) if you asked me.

"Hey Baby, we still on for tonight?" she asked with some sexy in her tone. After a short pause she said, "Okay, see you at ten then. You can pick me up at my house so I can just leave my car at home. No sense in both of us driving and I want to ride along with you anyway. Okay… Okay… Kisses!" She hung up.

"That bitch don't have no man. And if she do, then it sure the hell isn't Sledge. And why haven't we seen this mystery man at least once if he's so fuckin' special?"

Carmen didn't have any discretion and didn't care about the customers who were sitting there soaking up the drama between her and Selena, ready to run back and spread it through the town.

Always one to stir the pot, Bella said, "How you know he's not meeting her now, and *you* later?"

Carmen's neck turned in Bella's direction and cocked to the side… "Because he don't want that bitch, that's how. Watch this."

She called Sledge back, putting him on speaker…

"Baby, sorry to bother you again, are you busy?.... I just wanted to see if you could bring me a sandwich from Panera, something to hold me over until tonight. I didn't eat all day," she lied. Her ass been snacking all day. "And these little ass tea sandwiches aren't doing it for me."

"I'll be there in a little bit babe. I got you." Everybody heard him say.

He knew Selena worked here too and if he really comes here with food for Carmen, then I'd say it was clear who his choice was. Or else, he is just one foul ass dude who could care less about playing games with the both of their hearts – rubbing it in their faces that he doesn't give a fuck about either one of their feelings. I know damn well lil Ashlee was in here the other day telling me how she saw him and Selena eating together at Eat N Park – while ignoring Carmen's calls.

They hung up and twenty minutes later, he walked in with two brown Panera bags in one hand and a green tea for Carmen in the other. Carmen had just finished her client's hair and cashed her out. Her and Sledge went down to the lounge and ate their sandwiches and he sipped on a Corona while they talked.

I called down to let her know her next client was there. Carmen was satisfied with their little spontaneous meeting, secure in her thoughts that Selena wasn't with him and she was closer to that number one spot in his life. Maybe Selena does have a man and just enjoys messing with Carmen's head. I don't know – but hell, it's none of my business.

Past Mistakes

It was a very busy day, which meant Haji would be there for at least three to four hours. He was very thorough and worked alone, well at least here. He said he had six other contracts and had a team who helped him out with them. He was working this one by himself. I guess that's how Reese preferred it because this was a lot of work for one person, but I'm sure he was being paid well for taking it on alone.

Everyone had wrapped up for the day. Since I volunteered to lock up and was the only one still there once they all left, I decided to help him out by starting on the mirrors while I waited for him to get here. That's exactly what I was doing when he rang the buzzer. I hit the button from where I was standing, which was at Nel's station. He walked in looking delicious as always.

"You don't have to get your pretty little hands dirty Baby, I got this," he said, as he came closer, grabbing the bottle of Windex from my hand.

"Well, I've got nothing else to do, so I figured I'd help out. Why not?" I said, taking the bottle back from him. "I can do my own nails so I'm not worried about my hands."

He looked at my perfectly manicured nails, down to my matching pedicured toes, and back up at me with lust in his eyes. "Alright then, I won't argue with you. Let's get this done Baby."

~~~~~~~~

Over the next few weeks it became routine. I'd help him clean the shop every night and he'd take me home. We stopped and grabbed a bite to eat on several occasions and we even had a few drinks together at a few different bars. On one occasion it was Karaoke Night and since I was feeling a little tipsy, I sang him a song; "Unthinkable" by Alicia Keys, knowing if he asked me, I wasn't really ready. *Glad he didn't*! Only thing now is he asks me to sing for him all the time, saying I have a beautiful voice.

I was enjoying making the extra money. He was paying me for my help at the shop and MaKenzie and Reese were paying me for staying past normal business hours. It was considered overtime and the three of them were inflating my purse well, helping me save up for a car while still being able to help my grandmother with the bills. She's always talking about how she's on a *fixed income*. She doesn't pressure me or anything, but she hints around a lot.

Jax was still texting and calling and I was steady keeping things short with him, mainly when I was with dude. I loved him, but I wanted to love him as a friend and give my heart to someone else, preferably Haji.

Whenever Jax would call, we would make small talk and then I'd start an argument and he'd hang up on me. He grew tired of me throwing Shakira, his little girlfriend, up in his face every time we talked. He would start telling me how much he loves and misses me and how he wants me to be a permanent part of his life and every time I'd tell him it was all bullshit, especially as long as Lil Miss Thang was in the picture. He normally responded by saying, "All you have to do is say the word," but he got tired of repeating the same things and would just say "Bye" as soon as I would start my shit.

Part of me knew for a fact that he would drop her immediately if I changed my mind and decided to be with him in a committed relationship. Another part of me felt like it was best to let her keep him and deal with the bullshit that came along with the lifestyle he lived. Hell, I already knew what his sex was like. It was nothing short of amazing – but I was a young woman with a high sex drive and wasn't about to keep waiting around until he slid in to town to get some only to have to watch him leave me again. That shit is for the birds.

It's been a few weeks since the last time he's been here and the kitty wants to purr. I've only had sex with one other person besides him – *willingly*. That other guy just happens to be Lanel, the barber. It only happened once and we both knew it couldn't happen again and considered each other crazy for letting it happen in the first place.

See, Lanel has a little girl with MaKenzie's youngest sister. Her name is Autumn and they are getting married in September, a little over a month away.

When I first started working at MAD, he had already been working there for the last three years. He met Autumn when she came to visit her sister while she was on break from college one summer. MaKenzie liked Lanel and would have hand-picked him herself to date her sister – she thought he was very mature, a gentleman, and a young man with a keen business sense and a good head on his shoulders. As soon as the pair saw each other, MaKenzie didn't have to do or say a thing because they were attracted to each other from the jump. They are a match made in heaven and everyone, including myself, is genuinely happy for them.

Reese put him under his wing and they have been doing business together as far as real estate goes - buying and flipping houses and commercial properties. Lanel is good with his hands and renovates all the houses that Reese owns, turning them from shacks to lavish condos, townhouses and single-family homes. He even helped Reese build a couple mansions from the ground up and one of them Reese planned to move Makenzie into on their tenth wedding anniversary - which was next year.

I feel bad about our lil dirty deed, but I don't regret that it happened – its water under the bridge now and I do not plan on going there again – Autumn is sweet and doesn't deserve that, plus I like MaKenzie and wouldn't want to taint our friendship by hurting her sister. You know I'm blaming it on the alcohol, because it was present, heavily, in our systems at the time.

Two weeks after I started working there, MaKenzie threw a "Welcome Anitra" cocktail party at the shop. Apparently she had done this for everyone who joined the MAD Team. It was a Monday. I remember because it was an appointment day and MaKenzie told everyone not to schedule any after four o'clock so we could sit back and enjoy ourselves and have a few drinks – which we, as staff, were only allowed to partake in after our work day was over.

I mean, can you imagine the drunk fades and singed curls followed by lawsuits that would come up out of here if we drank while on the clock?

Makenzie would go off, but it was Reese who would fire every-damn-body if he thought we were doing that.

"That's a liability...which makes *you* a liability and because of that I would have to let you go...I don't care who you are," he said in a meeting once, saying he saw someone who would remain nameless, but they knew who they were, on the tapes having a beer during business hours.

Everybody knew he was talking about Juke. He felt since he was family he had job security.

Anyway, back to that day…

We sat around eating, listening to music, taking shots and laughing at Juke's corny jokes and the rip session between the fellas that ensued. Bella was cool from the jump and I guess Carmen had to feel me out before she opened up. She wasn't rude, but she didn't have too much rap for me and was actually the first to leave, taking Bella with her since they were friends and she was Bella's ride home. That was everybody else's cue to wind down and MaKenzie and the rest of the crew left shortly after them.

Lanel had ended up getting a call from one of his regulars who begged him for a quick cut because he was going out of town and had a flight to catch in less than three hours. I was enjoying myself so much that day that I wasn't ready to go home, so I asked Lanel if he could drop me off at a friend's house that didn't stay far from where he lived, adding that it was on the way to his house and wouldn't be much out of his way.

"Sure, I can do that… soon as I do this last cut. My mans is going out of town and want a fresh one real quick. Can you wait?"

"Yeah, of course I can. Thanks Nel."

I went down to the lounge and poured myself some Nuvo mixed with Ciroc. That was the drink that put me over the top – had one too many.

Lanel came downstairs to let me know he was ready because his boy changed his mind – he would have been cutting it close and didn't want to miss his flight. I didn't notice him

61

come down because I was too busy dancing with my eyes closed to Aaliyah's "Rock the Boat" that I had blasted on the system down there. I guess he was mesmerized by the way I was gyrating my hips and popping my ass – rocking the boat I was carrying on my backside. I caught him staring at my ass when I opened my eyes.

"Damn girl, you 'bout to get me in trouble."

I was feeling a bit tipsy and he was looking good over there with his soldier standing at attention through his shorts. There was about a minute left to the song as I made my way over, turning my back to him, dancing on his lap as he stood, grinding my ass back and forth across his erection. The song ended, breaking the moment.

"Damn girl, that lil number you just did got my dick hard as fuck. Let's get you to your destination before we do something we both may regret. Although… Never mind."

I wasn't trying to hear that. My inner nympho was preparing herself for what was about to take place – jumping up and down in the nude.

"What? Ain't no never mind. Say what you were going to say."

I was turned on. I had a thing for identifying everyone's celebrity look-alike and he favored Nelly's sexy ass to me. They look so much alike, you'd swear they were brothers if they were standing next to each other. The cat got his tongue as the next song came on and I began to dance again – seductively - like I do at home in the mirror. "Poppin" by Chris Brown was playing and it just happened to be one of the songs I loved to dance to. I put my hand around his neck and wrapped one of my legs around his waist, grinding my body against his. He *couldn't contain his libido as he leaned in to kiss me. That did it! We ended up having sex in one of the booths that was in the corner. He was working with something like an anaconda and I enjoyed every minute of it – Yup, all three minutes worth!*

"Damn you got some good pussy! I haven't had any all week cause my girl been away. She went to see her parents in Chicago," he explained. I laughed.

As if he'd immediately had an epiphany he yelled, "Fuck!" He jumped up out of the wetness that was me and pulled up his shorts and boxers in one swoop. "The cameras Nitra. The fucking cameras! MaKenzie is going to trip if she sees this on them damn tapes. Autumn will try to kill us both if she finds out."

We both sobered up real quick. It was so easy to forget the cameras were even there since you never see them. Add some liquor in the mix and discretion and reserve goes out the window and have you all caught up.

I was shitting bricks for the next few weeks just waiting for MaKenzie to confront me about the video. She never did. To this day, I'm not sure if she or Reese saw it because nothing ever came up about it from either one of them. I had asked Lanel if anyone said anything to him about it and he always said no and would tell me not to worry about it, "We're good." *Whatever that meant!* Yeah, we were definitely not doing that again. I just knew I was about to have some drama coming my way. I made sure to take the morning after pill because we didn't use a condom and I don't think he pulled out when he ejaculated. A baby with my boss' sister's fiancé was out of the question and I wasn't taking any chances. Yea – reckless on both our parts and won't be happening again – End of story! He is cool peoples but also someone else's property. Again – I want my own.

Change of Pace

Reese finally gave Haj a key and it seems as though that's when things started to change. I no longer needed to stay and close for them and that led to a shift in our normal routine. There were days I opted to do something else while he worked and there were days he'd insist I go home instead of helping him because I had already been on my feet all day. He was very considerate and sweet and never had a problem putting a smile on my face – whether it was through gifts or other displays of affection, or even just his words. My panties would be all in a hot bunch, on top of having a hungry anticipation for the day we would actually have sex.

I wanted him to be mine so I was exercising my strength, willing myself to hold off as long as I could. That's exactly why I always stayed in the truck whenever we stopped at his house to either drop something off or pick something up. I was afraid I'd give in if he got me to go in there. I almost melted every time he touched my leg, or even my damn shoulder, so I know I'd be putty in his hands if I did enter his home.

Jax was still the only man who has ever even seen the inside of my room and also the only man granted the chance to sex me in my bed. Whenever Haji and I chilled at my house, we didn't do much more than cuddle up in the family room on the couch while we watched movies.

Even my gram was starting to like him. She was all Team Jax not long ago. Now Haji Andrew Givner was winning over both our hearts. He was feeling me and I was feeling him – but he failed to mention I wasn't the only one.

It was nearing the end of July on a humid Friday night. Haji and I were on our way to my house after finishing up at the shop. We stopped at the gas station and he left his phone in the seat when he hopped out of the truck to pay for the gas. We've been talking for almost a couple months now and I wanted to see if there was any evidence of who he's fucking because I'm sure he has to be getting some from somewhere, especially since I hadn't given him any yet. Out of curiosity, I picked it up and went straight to his messages. For the sake of time, I clicked on the first one I saw. There was a trail of conversation between him and a woman stored as Chelle.

Chelle: Haji, we need to talk.

Him: Unless it involves business and/or my money, we have nothing to talk about.

Chelle: Really Haji!!!? You're going to put this all on me. We've both made mistakes. I'm willing to work on things and talk about it... Are you?

Him: No!!!!

The next message made my heart sink to my toes.

Chelle: So what?...You want a divorce? Is that what this means?

Hold Up! Hold Up! Hold Up! – Divorce? Did I just read that correctly? I read it again and yes, that's what it said. He came out of the store and I set the phone in the center console. He opened the door looking like he was searching for something. I turned and looked at him with tears in my eyes and pointed to his phone since we both knew that's what he was looking for. It's like he knew he'd fucked up and left some 'evidence' laying around. His eyes shifted in the direction of his phone and then back up at me.

A single tear fell from my eye, "You didn't tell me you were married Haji," I said through gritted teeth.

I was burning up on the inside; yet happy as hell I hadn't had sex with him yet. He looked back to his phone and back up at me for the second time and then spoke.

"That's because we're not together. We're separated."

"And you didn't think that was something I should know?"

"Well, yea... of course... I was just waiting for the right time. I didn't want to scare you off. I was going to tell you Nitra. I swear I was. We're getting a divorce, I just haven't told her yet. I went to see my lawyer yesterday."

"I don't believe you!" I burst out into tears, "I don't believe this shit. I'm glad I found out sooner rather than later. Your ass was supposed to tell me that in the beginning...Wasting my damn time."

I was livid to say the least.

"Will you let me explain?" He got in the truck and shut the door as two other cars pulled into the gas station, not wanting anyone to hear us argue.

"What's there to explain Haji? Separated or not, you have a wife and I've known nothing about her for damn near two months. You's a sneaky mother fucker! How'd you keep her, well me, a secret all this time? Take me the fuck home NOW!" I screamed.

He knew I was hot because I did my best to tame my potty mouth around him. He pulled out of the gas station and

66

started heading in the opposite direction of the way we are supposed to go to get to my house.

"Nah, we gon' talk about this shit."

I guess he had something to prove because he ignored my demands to turn this bitch around and instead he took me to his house.

As soon as we pulled up I yelled, "I'm not going in there. Do you share this house with your wife? … With…With Chelle or whatever the fuck her name is? Is that why you never pressured me to go in every time we stopped by here?"

He parked the truck in front of the door and cut the engine off, turning to look at me, letting out a big sigh.

"No Nitra. This is my house. I let her keep the house we lived in together and moved out and got my own. Get out the truck please. Let's go in here and talk. And for the record, I didn't pressure you because I was waiting for you to be comfortable enough to come in on your own. You've always been welcome. You refused the first time I asked and I just never asked again."

I folded my arms across my chest.

"I really don't want to hear shit you have to say. I just want to go home. But then again, I feel like you owe me – you owe me the truth. I'm sure after tonight we're done because I don't want no other woman's damn husband. Fuck I look like? I play second to none. And it's wrong, it's just wrong."

He wasn't taking no for an answer. He got out and walked around to my side, opening the door – "Get out the truck Nitra. If you're not going to do it willingly then I'm going to drag your ass out of there. You are not leaving here until we talk about this. What? You want me to call the bitch right now. It's obvious you read the messages. I told her ass I don't have shit to say to her. Come on man... let's just go in the house. It's humid as hell out here."

I got out the truck and slammed the door shut as hard as I could, hoping to shatter the glass of his window. This mother fucker had the nerve to smile at me and chuckle like he found the shit funny. He walked ahead of me, pulling out his keys and unlocking the door to the house.

Upon entering the door, we were met with two sets of stairs. One leading down to what I guess is the basement and the other leading to the upper level of the house. We went up the steps leading from the entrance to the living room, which we bypassed and went straight to his bedroom. We passed by the kitchen, dining room, two other bedrooms and a bathroom along the way.

I noted as I walked by how neat, clean and artistically decorated it was throughout his three-bedroom, two- bath, ranch-style bachelor pad. Everything looked expensive and I began to wonder just how much he was worth and what other 'business' he had going on. I'd always seen him in his 'work clothes' except for a few occasions where he'd stopped by the house on my off day to chill with me or take me out to eat somewhere or see a movie, which we'd only done twice. Even then, he was casual. He drove a brand new black and red F-150 with black rims, trimmed with red lining, but I figured he could afford it because he was a man who worked hard.

I'm not really concerned with how much money he has though. I really enjoy his company and conversation and how he treats me like the queen that I am. He is a good listener and a very intelligent man. Based on all the talks we've had and the books along the wall-length book shelf I saw as we passed the dining room, I can tell that he possessed more than just street knowledge. His aura is one that commands respect and I've witnessed his ability to break someone down with his vocabulary and intellect alone – without ever raising his voice or losing his cool. *"Intelligence is so sexy,"* I thought to myself.

I was impressed stepping into his bedroom. Everything was black and white with gray splashed throughout. It was very spacious with high ceilings and thick, fluffy, black carpet, four arched windows and did I say lots of space.

"I'm going to take a shower first and get out of these work clothes and then we'll talk." He said, stopping to look me in my face.

I shot him an evil look and rolled my eyes, "Yeah, Whatever."

He removed his fitted baseball cap and set it and his keys on top of the longest dresser I'd ever seen, ignoring my attitude, and went to take his shower. I so wanted to go in there with him but that is not happening because I am so mad, No – I'm *Hot* right now!

You could tell this was where he spent most of his time. Everything you would need or want was right here in this room, including a huge bathroom and since he's taking a shower at the moment, I'm not going in there. I'll see what he got going on up in that piece later – well soon, because I have to pee, but not until he comes out. Just think… he's naked…wet, toned, hung and yea, naked.

Yes, I admit, I've been teasing him lately and got a chance to feel him up and Um, yea, let's just say that 90 day rule Steve Harvey told me about in his book – ummm, I won't be making that. Shit – it's been 43 days or so since I've had *any*… Close enough in *my* book!

Mmmmmh… *"Girl, you better contain yourself. We out of here in less than an hour and I got you. I'll even buy some new batteries, full power, but not tonight heffa – We gotta make him sweat for this bullshit. A damn wife and I didn't know about her. Nah, he ain't getting shit tonight. Soon though, girl, soon!"*

I had to calm the kitty. It took on a voice of its own in my head. Feisty little bitch when she's horny.

"Vitamin D for dick deficient, Bitch… Them AA's aren't doing it for me" she cried.

I made a deal with her. *"Tomorrow."*

One more day wouldn't hurt – but definitely not tonight. The sex goddess in my head finally took a seat on my cerebrum, crossing her legs, pouting while fighting the sexual tension, but accepting the terms of our agreement.

So far, I was digging him and his style and was thinking I could get spoiled, fast, if I stayed too long as I looked around at my current surroundings. Whatever he has to say better be good, or else there will have to be a breach in the contract I'd just made with the nympho inside of me.

A black refrigerator, that stood about five feet tall, more slender than wide, sat in the far right corner in the back of the room. That section was squared off with over-sized, Italian, black leather furniture. A black marble table with metallic gray sparkles glistening on the surface was resting on top of a gray, black and white rug in the center of the area. A 72" flat screen TV was mounted on the wall and could be seen and enjoyed from the comfort of his king-size bed. It sat directly across from it, to the far left side of the room – depending on where you were standing of course. If you were in the area where the couches and TV was, it would be the far right, but walking in the entrance to his bedroom – it would be to your left.

I powered on the tell-lie-vision as he once called it, turning to B.E.T. to watch some videos while I waited. The speakers that were mounted on the walls around the room gave it a theatre-type appeal.

I took my shoes off and walked to his bed and laid down in the middle of it. It was very comfortable as I laid there and became engrossed in my thoughts. Thoughts of him, this Chelle chick and the situation at hand.

I thought of my gram and how she's been getting sicker and sicker by the day and I even thought about Jax and his lil – whatever, wondering how close the two had become since I basically stopped answering his calls completely.

I really wanted to forget about Haji and his wife for the time being and have him all for myself, even if only for tonight… but I yelled at the freak in my head again and told her to sit her lil hot ass down. *"Quit acting like a bitch in heat. I said To-morrow."* I had to at least make him pay somehow and that meant – *No pussy for him tonight.* He's going to wait a little while longer for this. Shit, he might just be waiting forever.

After a good twenty minutes, he emerged from the bathroom, steam following behind him as he exited, with a navy blue towel wrapped around his waist – exposing his muscular calves and toned upper body. He headed straight to his extra-long dresser, opening a drawer and pulling out some boxers and another pulling out some white socks and then a different one, grabbing up a white wife beater. *Waaay too organized for me.*

71

He knew what the fuck he was doing. He was trying to distract me with his dick that was hanging as he un-wrapped the towel, letting it fall to the floor as he stepped into his boxers.

Decisions, Decisions...

My eyes zeroed in on his dick and I had to look away. That thing looked like a long cucumber dipped in milk chocolate. "Mmm, *I Love Chocolate!*", I said, hungrily in my head. "*Focus, Nitra, Focus!*" I had to tell myself. He walked over to the bed where I had now sat up, sitting on the edge watching every sexy ass move he made.

He proceeded to put on his socks and then his beater as he began to speak, "Nitra, baby, I don't want her. It's over and she knows it. I will call her right now if you want me to and tell her that shit – for the umpteenth time. That bitch ain't shit and I don't know why I married her in the first place. Well, yes I do, but that's neither here nor there."

I turned the power to the TV off, giving him my undivided attention… Well, almost. My eyes kept wandering to that chocolate eye peeking at me through the slit in his boxers as he sat down with his legs outstretched and his back against the headboard. I wanted to tell his ass to cover that thing up but instead I tried my best to ignore it.

"Huh? What does that mean? Why did you marry her if she "ain't shit?", I asked doing the little "quote, unquote" sign with my hands.

He motioned for me to come to him. I did, laying my back to his chest. *Why did I do that? I feel…secure here.* As mad as I was, it felt good to feel my body up against his.

He answered, "She was pregnant."

I sat up and swung my neck around to look him in the face, "So you have a child too? What the fuck Haji?"

"No. No, I don't have a child. The baby was stillborn. That was two years ago. When she told me she was pregnant with my seed, I decided to make her my wife and give my child a family, a real one - complete with both parents. Settle down and do the right thing, you know? Things didn't work out that way though. Ain't no telling what that bitch was doing while she was pregnant with my son. How the fuck you carry a baby for nine months and it come out dead? Needless to say, shit hasn't been the same since. We've been separated for a little over a year now. I wasn't in love with her when I married her and I damn sure am not in love with her now. What we had is over. I want you to be my wife."

He leaned forward and started rubbing his hands up and down my breasts, making my nipples perk up in anticipation. I put my hands over his, trying to stop him from arousing me any further.

"Sorry to hear about your son," I said sincerely. I heard the pain in his voice when he spoke about his son and it caused me to speak in a soft tone. "I'm still mad at you for not telling me about her in the beginning. And don't even go there. We haven't even known each other long enough for you to want me to be your wife. Plus, if I'm not mistaken, isn't it illegal to get married while you're still married to someone else? There's a name for that you know? And it comes with a charge. Talking 'bout marrying me and you haven't even cut loose from the first one yet."

"Yeah, but I *am* divorcing her. ASAP! I told you I went to see my lawyer yesterday. Her ass is going to be served with them papers real soon. Just some lil loose ends I have to tie up first. I don't care if it's only been two months – I'm feeling you.

74

I'm falling in love with you and I haven't even got no pussy yet. It's just something about your lil young ass. You are wise beyond your years. And such a fuckin' lady. Classy not trashy and I want you to be mine. All mine. I want you to be my woman. Let's make it official Nitra."

"I don't think so Haji. I told you I'm not playing second to nobody, plus, I don't want to get my feelings hurt. That's why I left Jax's ass alone. You say you don't love her, haven't loved her in a long time and have been separated for over a year – yet you're just now supposedly starting divorce proceedings. You have to be still connected to her for a reason. What is it? Sexually? Emotionally?... I want somebody for myself. I'm not into the sharing thing."

"You don't have to share Nitra. I just asked you to be my number one. I'm all yours right now. I'm done with Michelle. I just wish she'd get it through that thick ass head of hers that I don't want her anymore. I want you. Okay, so I'm not divorced yet, but I haven't even been living with her for over a year now. That has to count for something. I'm not out to hurt your feelings. Give me some rope! Trust me and the only thing that will be hanging is our wedding portrait on the wall."

He got up and laid me backwards, getting on top of me and planting a long, passionate kiss on my lips. He started unbuttoning my pants and lifting my shirt as he continued kissing me, moving from my lips to my neck and all the way down to my navel. Ms. Nympho starting doing flips as I shut down the celebration once again, pushing him off of me and started buttoning my pants back up.

His phone started buzzing over on the dresser. "It's probably your wife. Take me home Haji. Please? I just need some time to take this all in and think for a moment."

"Come on baby, don't do that to me. We don't have to do anything, just stay the night with me. I'm not done *talking* to you." His phone stopped and started again. "Go head boo, how about you answer it for me."

I took him up on his offer and got up to answer his phone.

"Hello, Haji's phone, how may I help you?"

"You can help by putting my husband on the phone bitch. Who the fuck is this?" She came through with much attitude in her tone.

"Um, the names Anitra, not Bitch, but if you must, it's Ms. Bitch to you." Haji's eyes grew wide, and then he smiled at me and started nodding his head.

"Well Ms. Bitch, put my husband on the phone. The fuck you answering his shit for anyway?"

"He told me to, *that's* why. Evidently you are no longer the woman he wants. That would be me! But, I'll let you speak to your soon-to-be ex-husband just this once so he can tell you himself." I handed him the phone, taking a seat on the bed to see how this was going to play out.

"What Michelle?" He listened for a second and said, "Fuck No and Fuck You!... That's none of your fucking business... Nah Nope, this shit with us is done." He paused for a moment more, "Yeah, yeah, whatever... show me some proof." He ended the call. "Now do you believe me? Stay with me Nitra."

"Show you some proof about what? What did she say?"

"Nothing. She's a fucking liar and just mad cause you answered my phone. Fuck her!"

He pulled me closer and started kissing me again. It felt so good as he ran his hands up the inside of my thighs, forcing two fingers up my shorts and inserting them into my love nest.

"Mmmm, Haj, stop."

I was starting to breathe heavy as I felt my strength to fight getting weaker and weaker, succumbing to the sensation his fingers were giving me as he massaged my clit in a circular motion.

"Take these shorts off. Let me taste her."

I stood up, giving in, and took my shorts off. He did the honors of removing my thong and then my shirt and bra. I stood there naked as my inner nympho was fanning the fire igniting my insides. *"Fuck it, 43 days it is. It's going down tonight. You win! Happy now Bitch!"* She shook her head up and down rapidly as he laid me down in the middle of his bed, climbing in between my legs. His phone started buzzing again. We ignored it.

He licked my clit once and then blew on it, inserting three fingers this time. He went in and went to work, driving me up the length of his bed using his tongue until I couldn't take it anymore, head now resting on the headboard, giving him a look that said, *"What the fuck are you trying to do to me?"* Tears rolled down my eyes as he brought me to climax. I never felt like this before. Jax was good, but not this fucking good!

It was over once he came up and starting kissing me, slowly inserting his nine inch dick, giving it all to me little by little until it felt like he was all the way in my stomach.

"Oooh, Haj, go sloooow. Ooooh, you're so …. Big. Go slow…. Mmmmm."

He did as I asked and only began to speed up and pump harder as he was about to cum.

"Oh my … girl, this pussy is so good… Damn!"

He closed his eyes tight and came all up inside me. I'm like, *oh no, not another three minute man.* He shut me the fuck up when he turned me over, dick still rock hard and started hitting it from the back. He started out slow and then gradually sped up. The force of each thrust and the sound of our bodies clapping had me going insane. I shook my head violently from side to side, and then dropped my head low and lifted it back up again – repeating these motions as I gripped the pillow tight. He occasionally smacked me on the ass, his palm laying fire on each cheek, intensifying the experience. I came again and so did he, and he still wasn't done. He turned me on my side, lifting my leg in the air and started grinding round and round, working the middle something serious – that shit felt un-fucking-believable. He turned me every which way as we fucked for at least forty five minutes to an hour straight. *Or did we just make love?* I was exhausted once we were done.

We hadn't even caught our breaths yet when his phone started buzzing again. Now, this bitch was really about to get cussed out. After the way he just turned me out – I'm stating my claim on that. This is my dick for now on.

I picked up his phone and he had a message. I opened it up and it was a picture of a pregnancy test with two pink lines, indicating it was positive. The bitch done killed my groove. I got up and started putting my clothes on and threw his phone at him.

78

"What the fuck Nitra… Where are you going?"

"There's your fucking proof Haji. Take me home or I'll walk. Either way, I'm getting the fuck out of here."

He looked at the message and threw his phone against the wall, cracking the screen. "Fuck!" He screamed. "This is some bullshit. She's not pregnant. And if she is, I'm sure it's not by me with her grimy ass. She's playing games. She's full of lies Nitra. "

"Yeah, yeah, Whatever. You obviously still fucking her if there's even a possibility so save the bullshit. You got what you wanted. Now take me home."

I was so angry and hurt. He knew I would walk like I said I would so he put his clothes on and took me home. We rode in silence the whole way there. As we pulled up, I immediately noticed Jax's car parked in front of Leslie's house across the street. *"Dammit, could this night get any worse"*, I said under my breath. My heart dropped. I know he's here because I have been ignoring the shit out of him the last few weeks. Not accepting any of his calls or returning any of his messages. He wanted answers and I really didn't feel like dealing with him, especially while I'm already heated with this mother fucker right here.

"Nitra, I'm sorry. Can I see you tomorrow so we can finish this discussion? I know this bitch isn't pregnant and if she is, it's not by me. Please believe me. She play them childish games all the time and she's probably only saying that cause you answered my phone and she want to start some shit. That's what she does. It's who she is and I could kick myself for the total lapse in judgment for ever fucking with her dumb ass."

As far as I was concerned, there was nothing to discuss.

"I saw the fucking test with my own two eyes Haji. It's over. I don't have this shit to do."

I got out the car and slammed the door once again and took flight in the house, crying as I slammed yet another door – Mine – right in his face as he was walking fast behind me, "Nitra, how is it over and we just getting started. I can show you better than I can tell you if you just give me a chance."

I screamed through the door, "Just go away."

Truth is, I wanted to let him show me, but right now he needed to go. I saw Leslie's door open, which meant Jax knew I was home and I was sure he was on his way over here. No telling what he's going to do or what frame of mind he's in and I don't need no chalk and yellow tape outside me and my grandma's home.

I decided to wait to talk to Haji and I was so relieved that he pulled off without putting up too much of a fight.

Kidnap or Surrender...

My grandma was still in the living room, which was odd because it was three o'clock in the morning. "What's the matter baby? He do something to you?" She had been in the window since we pulled up.

"Nothing grandma. No, he didn't do anything but turn out to be a jerk. What you still doing up anyway?" I said, wiping my tears away with the back of my hand.

"Jayson was here. He just left a good twenty minutes ago. He was trying to wait for you. He went across the street to that girl's house you be over. He said to call him when you got here."

Knock, knock, knock.

"That must be him", she said.

I opened the door and immediately went in on him, "What the hell you got my grandma up this time of the morning for? Boy is you crazy? What do you want Jax?"

"I want you. What's wrong Nee Nee? Why you been crying? That nigga do something to you? I'll kill his ass."

He said that shit with much conviction, ignoring my hostility.

"No, nobody done anything to me. And watch your mouth." I told him, remembering my gram was still in the room.

He looked over my shoulder and saw my granny still sitting there, "Oh… Sorry, Ms. Lorene. It's just I'll hurt somebody about her."

Little did she know, he was serious as cancer and would definitely do more than hurt somebody – he would *kill* someone and not just about me. I try to tell her she doesn't know him like I know him. She's been watching him grow up since he was a child and always felt he was so respectful that she wouldn't believe me if I told her. *"Maybe if I did, she would stop trying to push me on him, trying to be Ms. Matchmaker,"* I thought to myself.

"Don't I know it", she responded to him, "I'm going to bed now. You two be good."

She made her way up the steps huffing and puffing and coughing the whole time.

Jax hollered behind her as he pushed pass me and went to the bottom of the steps, "Ms. Lorene. Is it okay if I take Nitra out of town for a couple of days to show her my new condo? It sure could use a woman's touch. My mother said she can stay here with you or at least check on you every day until I bring her back."

I looked at him like he was crazy.

"What? I'm not going anywhere with you. Grandma, don't pay him any mind." I screamed up at her, pulling him back into the living room.

My grandma spoke up, "Nitra, I think you should go. I'll be alright for a couple of days. You know Joyce will check on me while you're away. Go on and take you a break for a few days. All you do is work, work, work." She said from the top of the stairs.

"Nitra, just come with me for a few days, that's all I'm asking for. You even have your grandma's blessing." He lowered his tone. "Don't make me drag you the fuck up out of here. At this point, I'm done playing with your ass."

He pulled me onto the porch and shut the door so my gram couldn't hear him threatening me. "You're coming whether you want to or not. You promised you would visit soon and now is the time. You haven't been answering my fucking calls. Haven't returned any of my messages. What? You think a nigga was going for that shit. I told you, you are mine forever. And you agreed remember. So I tell you what – It's kidnap or surrender – which is it gonna be?"

I really didn't feel like arguing with him, plus I was pissed at Haji and didn't want to see him for a while anyway. I needed to let his ass sweat for a couple days.

I actually knew this day was coming. I know Jax like the back of my hand, although I was quite surprised he didn't come sooner.

He wasn't taking no for an answer, so I agreed to go, "Fine! I surrender. You got it. I'll go, but only for a few days."

I packed a bag with some of my belongings and Jax and I hit the road a half an hour later. I kissed my grandma before I left and promised to call her when we got there. I texted MaKenzie, letting her know I wouldn't be at work for a while and that I'd let her know what was going on soon. It was late, so I didn't expect a reply. I just didn't want to forget to let her know.

Getting away for a while is just what I needed right now because I couldn't think straight. I slept the whole ride to Maryland, unable to keep my eyes open because they were so heavy from crying.

~~~~~~~~~~

I woke up the following morning in another state and in another man's bed. I opened my eyes to unfamiliar surroundings as it took my brain a minute to catch up. I sat up and scanned the room until my eyes landed on a clock that sat on a night stand on the other side of the bed. It was almost nine thirty. I haven't slept this late in a long while. My body was basically programmed to wake up at six-thirty in the morning.

I heard voices coming from a television outside the door. I hopped out of the bed and headed in the direction of the noise, stopping off at the bathroom in the hallway that lead to the living room and the rest of the small, yet cozy one bedroom apartment. As I sat down to pee, Jax knocked once on the bathroom door and then let himself in.

"Uh, I'm in here," I said as if that wasn't obvious. *This fool is too damn comfortable. I mean, I know it's nothing he never seen before but can a lady have some damn privacy?*

"Duh," he responded, handing me a wash cloth, towel and a brand new toothbrush still in its packaging. "Toothpaste is in the medicine cabinet. Take care of that morning breath so I can get a kiss and then get yourself together so we can go have some brunch."

He left back out, closing the door behind him. I locked it so that he couldn't invade my privacy again while I took a shower. I got in and turned the water on steaming hot, standing up under the shower head to allow the water to drown out my tears and my silent cries as I started thinking about Haji.

I remembered this was the first chance I got to wash the juices off my body from the amazing sex we had the night before. I had powered my phone off once Jax and I got on the road and I'm certain he has been trying to call me all night. I need to leave well enough alone while I still have the chance, but for some reason, I still wanted to be with him.

After about fifteen minutes, Jax knocked on the door, breaking me from my thoughts. "Nee, Baby, let's go. A nigga hungry as hell."

So was I so I yelled, "Okay, I'll be out in a second."

After another ten minutes or so I got out, wrapping the over-sized towel around my body and went back in his room to get dressed. I was sitting on the bed, rubbing lotion over my body when I heard the house phone ring. I ear hustled a little and from the sound of the conversation, I figured it was little Ms. Shakira who must not have been too happy when he told her I was here. I heard him tell her to "Stop tripping". There is about to be trouble in paradise once she finds out I'll be staying here, sleeping in his bed for the next couple days. But shit, no worries, she can have his ass. I didn't want to be here no way, but I also didn't feel like fighting with his simple ass. I only agreed to come to appease him and get him off my back – and of course make Mr. "I have a damn wife" sweat for a couple days.

I got my outfit together and laid it across the bed. I retrieved my cell from my purse and powered it back on. I had ten new voicemails and five text messages. Seven of the voicemails were of course from Haji, begging me to call him. I had one from MaKenzie letting me know she got my text and telling me to give her a call when I got a chance. The other two were from friends; one from Leslie, my neighbor and the other was from LaDawna, my best friend. I hadn't talked to Dawn in a minute so I made a mental note to call her after we ate so her and I could catch up. No matter how long we went without talking to each other, our friendship was strong as ever. I planned to call Leslie anyway to ask her personally to check up on my grandmother for me every now and then while I'm away for these couple of days. I'll call both of these ladies after we handle our business for the day and I have some time to pow wow.

I need *somebody* to talk to about my situation and it damn sure couldn't be Jax. *Picture that*! He's not trying to hear that. Me, talking about another man to him – Nah, not happening. I don't need that explosion. It would more than likely be Dawn I talk to about it. She is my long-time friend and confidant. As much as I like Leslie, she is Ms. Mouth of the South, living on the North and I only told her what I wanted her to know. She not going have my business plastered around the city. She is usually the one doing all the talking anyway and I just suck up all her gossip like a sponge. That girl got more drama than H.B.O. going on in her life alone, add to that the stories she tell about everything going on in the hood and you have your very own blockbuster right there. I could write a book about her life and her stories and get paid! – *Hmmmm*.

I powered my phone back off, got dressed and went in the living room where Jax was sitting on an ottoman, puffing on a blunt and finishing up his phone call. Seems the only time I smoked was when I was with him or over at Leslie's. He passed it to me as he said his goodbyes. As soon as he ended the call he stood up, licking his lips as he looked at me with love and lust in his eyes.

Then, out of the blue he says, "I can't believe you fucked that nigga. You gave my pussy away."

That caught me off guard. I didn't know what to say. I took another puff, inhaled and exhaled and put it out in the ashtray.

"What? What are you talking about Jax?"

He walked up on me, his face all up in mine with that look of love and lust suddenly turning to disdain, "Don't play stupid Nitra. We both know you smarter than that and I'm not a dumb nigga either. I probably know your body better than you do. I also know how you smell and you had another nigga's scent all over you. I put my fingers in that pussy last night, ready to get some of that and wake you up to some of this good dick until I pulled them out, ready to taste your juice on my fingers, and smelled them. I knew instantly someone been up in my shit."

I wasn't feeling his tone, his screw-face or the fact that he then grabbed me by the back of my hair, jerking my neck back some and asked me through gritted teeth, "So what happened? You gave that nigga some ass Nee? Tell the truth or I'll snap your fucking neck."

Oh, he got me fucked up! Tears instantly welled up in my eyes. "Get your mutha fuckin' hands off of my hair and let me the fuck go and then you are taking me home. I know you didn't bring me here so you could man handle me and shit. And you are not my man mother fucker! I told you I could do what I want. Why you going do this and fuck up our friendship? You know what - Fuck you – I see now that you are not my fucking friend at all, so I damn sure don't want you as my man – you can forget that. And especially not after this bullshit here. Let my hair go Jax," I screamed.

87

He let my hair go and I smacked the shit out of him. This sick bastard smirked at me like it didn't faze him at all and had the nerve to grab me by my arms, lock me in place and he started to kiss me. I kept moving my head violently from left to right trying to get his lips the fuck off of me. He held me tighter and threw his tongue in my mouth and down my throat and dammit the shit felt so good. I stopped fighting since I wasn't doing anything but making him grip me tighter anyway and let him kiss me. He is such a good kisser and it felt really good, too good for the situation. It lasted for a minute and then he released me from his grip.

He started laughing, "That's why I love you. You don't put up with my bullshit. Feisty and I love it."

I smacked the shit out of him again and a little harder this time. He then kissed me with the back of his hand, busting me in my bottom lip, "That don't mean you going keep putting your fucking hands on me."

I was hot now, tears flowing and I started screaming at him some more, "Fuck You! The fuck you mean? Fuck You! You the one all pulling on my hair and shit! I told you not to ever threaten me again, and putting your hands on me is a definite no-no and now you've done both. I hate you for that and I will never respect you again. I just lost *all* respect for you Jax. That's some bitch ass shit you just pulled. You ain't no man and I want to go home."

I stood there with my arms folded across my chest, bouncing my leg up and down, with tears flowing rapidly, threatening to make a puddle in the middle of the floor at the rate they were falling.

"I'm not taking you no-fuckin'-where! We agreed you were mine forever remember? You fucked that lame so that means you in violation."

Come Again! – This fool done lost his damn mind!

"Really Jax? Are you fucking serious right now? Ok, fine. I'll make my own fucking way home. You can't make me stay here. And hold up… don't you have a fucking girlfriend?. Wasn't that just your bitch on the phone? The fuck you sweating me for? You just blew damn near ten years of friendship right down the drain. I can't believe this."

I went to grab my purse and pull out my phone. He beat me to it and took my phone out and removed the battery. I really don't have the energy for this bullshit. I was basically surrendering at that moment because I was so hurt and I just couldn't take anymore. So hurt by what had just happened between me and a man I thought would never hurt me – intentionally – and definitely not physically.

My thoughts turned to Haji once more, and again, I felt hurt by yet another man – the one whom I really wanted to be with, just the night before – and not to mention after some of the best sex I've had in my life.

Yup – I'm in love! I had to laugh at myself on that one. You know there's something about some good dick ladies – lol! No, but for real, he makes me happy, he kept a smile on my face and treats me like a queen – always making me feel special and dear to his heart. You would think Anita named me Beautiful at birth as much as he called me that every day.

I started feeling like perhaps I was over-reacting just based on those facts alone. From the day we met, we've spent so much time together that he really hasn't had much time to be seeing anyone else – not even his wife. We've pretty much been inseparable since day one and now I just want to get home and at least talk to him.

I want to talk to him. I need to talk to him... but of course this fool just took my phone *and* disconnected his house phone from the wall so I couldn't call a cab or anybody else for that matter.

He cut off my thoughts by opening his mouth and instantly made me sick to my stomach.

"Your grandma is the only person you need to be communicating with and she can reach you on my phone."

He said that shit like he could read my thoughts. I decided to just go along with things for now. I was totally out of oomph to continue arguing with his stupid ass.

"Whatever", I said dryly with a tear-stained face.

I had stopped crying once I got to thinking about my grandmother and how once I get home to her, he would become a friend of my past. I ran in his room, locking the door behind me and laid in his bed to think and cry, and think and cry some more.

He came to the door actually trying to apologize, "Nee. I'm sorry baby... Can you unlock the door so we can talk? Damn! I know I fucked up and I feel fucked up for putting my hands on you. I honestly lost it... just at the thought of me possibly losing you to someone else... when I've been wanting you for myself all these years. Whatever I got to do to make this shit up to you, I'm willing to do it. I'm so sorry."

I heard everything he was saying but I ignored him. I don't have no rap for him at all right now. And definitely wasn't trying to hear none of that bullshit he was saying from behind that door. I'm no priest and this isn't a fucking confession booth so he can take that shit elsewhere. At this moment, my heart was saying, "*God forgives, I don't!*"

I then immediately started praying for forgiveness and help with forgiving and hoped that the Lord understood. I was in pain right now and wasn't quite in a forgiving mood.

I guess he decided to let me have my space because I heard the door slam. Since I had no phone, no car, and didn't know anyone or my way around here, I decided against attempting to leave while he was out. I was bout tired as shit and worn out at this point. I decided I was going to give him his "few days" and then I would be out of his life forever. I laid there and I thought and cried until I eventually cried myself to sleep.

"I Can Love You Better"

Selena

I had called MaKenzie at seven this morning to tell her I wouldn't be in *again*. I have two very important things on my agenda for today. Number one being a special trip to see my ob./gyne to confirm what I already knew.

I've missed two periods already and figured I had to be at least two and a half months along. Add to that the fact that I've been missing a lot of work due to severe morning sickness and just being downright tired, lacking the energy to do anything, especially being on my feet all damn day doing hair. I'd say I was definitely knocked up.

The second and most important thing I couldn't wait to tackle was her husband.

I know it's wrong but I don't care. I'm in love with Maurice Dixon and I'm going to have his baby. I'm kind of nervous about telling him, but I need to get it out of the way and tonight is the night.

I'm prepared for his initial reaction – which will be to think of MaKenzie and his children and how this is going to change everything for all of them if I keep it. All I know is, however he responds to the news, I'm keeping my child – end of story.

My time at his wife's business is about to come to a close anyway, thanks to him, so the conflict there is settled. In a minute, I'll be working in a shop I can call my own. It's not laid out like hers, but it's mine and he's paying for it and that's all that matters to me.

He had one of his properties renovated and turned it into "Hair Magic", the name I'd chosen for my new establishment. The only downside was that it is located in Wexford – clear on the other side of town than MAD, where all my clients reside. He ain't slick; He's trying to get me as far away from *her* as possible. I'm cool with that though. *Works for me!*

I'm confident that most of my clientele will follow and sure that I'll gain some new clients in my new location. I plan to hire two stylists so the shop can remain open when it comes time to deliver my baby.

Speaking of my baby, let me get my ass up and get moving so I can go check on the little bun in the oven. My appointment is at 10:30.

~~~~~~~~~

I arrived at my appointment ten minutes early, signed in and took a seat while I waited to be registered. A Homely Homes magazine was sitting on the table next to me, so I picked it up and started flipping through the pages, getting ideas on decorating my new pad which was conveniently located above my new salon. There were so many color schemes and different gadgets and styles of furniture, including some cute stuff for children in there that I decided to stuff it in my purse so I could make a collage of the things I liked later.

Fifteen minutes had passed and I was registered and called to the back so I could meet with Dr. Sendrict.

She checked my pulse, my temperature, my blood pressure and had me step on the scale. To my surprise, I had already put on eight pounds since my last visit. If this was any indication to the weight I stood to gain throughout this pregnancy, I'd better retain a personal trainer now.

The time came for me to pee in the cup and wait on my confirmation and sure enough, ten minutes later, my pregnancy was confirmed. Based on the date of my last period, Dr. Sendrict set my due date for February 7th – exactly a month before Maurice and MaKenzie's 'renewing of their vows".

That is, if they make it that far. I'm certain she is not going to handle this bombshell too well. I want to give him the chance to man up and tell her himself once he knows, but he better tell her soon. She will know one way or another even if I have to tell her myself.

Depending on how tonight goes when I tell him the news – his actions will determine my reaction and the next steps I choose. (Insert devilish grin here!)

I got my prescription for prenatal vitamins and iron pills, set my follow up appointment and got out of there to get ready for my date with my baby tonight. As soon as I left the building, I was so excited that I took a 'selfie' pic, donning my brightest smile and posted it to Instagram and Facebook simultaneously. I captioned it "Glowing". I dropped my phone in my purse and headed to my car.

Even though I knew I was pregnant – even though I knew my body was changing and there was a baby growing inside – having it confirmed by my Gyne elated me even more. For me, it was the stamp that made it official.

I got in my ride feeling good, immediately changing the song on the mixed cd to number seven. It was my jam and also my baby's ringtone. I turned it up and sang along as I pulled off… "I can love you, I can love you, I can love you better than she can." *Mary J. is that Chick! Love her music!*

MaKenzie

Don't get caught looking left
When you should be looking right.
Shit hiding in plain sight,
Yet you've become so preoccupied with looking in the wrong direction
to see the Light.

It was a full house, minus Anitra, and I had my "Do Not Disturb" sign hanging outside my office door. Speaking of Nitra, she hasn't been here in four days. She texted me on Friday, well Saturday morning, saying she wouldn't be at work for a while and was going to let me know what was going on soon. I was beginning to worry about her. That child is about her money and never takes off more than a day at a time, and that doesn't happen too often. She's always the first one on the job every day of the week.

I asked Haji if he knew anything about what was going on with her or if he'd at least heard from her and knows if she's alright. We talked in length and he told me everything that had happened between them the night she basically decided to disappear.

I kind of got the feeling she's with that damn Jax. He was all she talked about before ol' boy came in the picture. She's told me so much about him and the shit he's into that I can't help but to worry and hope he hasn't forced her to leave against her will or something.

When I asked Haji if he knew anything, he said he'd been by her house and all her grandmother will tell him is that she is with a "friend of the family." He's so sweet that he's been going over there checking up on Nitra's grandma every day since she's been gone. Of course, I know a major part of that is because he's hoping to see Nitra when she decides to come home, but it's still nice of him to look out for her gram in the meantime. He says she's quite sick – which is another reason I'm worried about baby girl. She loves her grandma and would be floored if anything happened to her in her absence. I can't see her staying away too long. It's been almost a week since anyone, I guess besides her grandmother, has heard from her and something just doesn't feel right to me about the whole situation.

I wanted to tell Haji who I thought this "friend of the family" was but felt it wasn't my place and that Nitra probably just needed some time to calm down. She was probably just being stubborn because she got her little feelings hurt. But shit, I'd be hurt too if the man I was falling for had a whole wife that I didn't know about. Even I was shocked when he told me that one. She wants a love of her own and doesn't want to be someone's side chick, and definitely doesn't want to interfere with a union brought before God. I know that about her. We've had the conversation plenty of times. She is truly a good person and that's why I like her.

Some broads don't think like that and always wanting something that doesn't belong to them. They stop at nothing to get with the next woman's man, lurking in the shadow of their heart's desires with ill intentions, trying to wreck some shit, thinking it's some type of game. At least Haji is separated and filing for a divorce. If I was Nitra, I'd go for it. Why should she deny her chance at love if he's not going to be with the woman anyway? He adores Nitra and as far as I'm concerned, he is by far better for her than that damn Jax.

My husband and I have been married for almost ten years – together for twelve – and believe me when I tell you, he makes me so happy. Well, he used to. I thought he was happy too until I found out that he is nothing but a big fucking liar. I got something for him though, and especially one bitch in particular. None of these women he's out here sleeping around with can wear my last year's panties, but with her – Oh, it's personal! I got caught looking left with her, when the shit has been right in my face the whole time.

So far I've been gathering my evidence but I'm not done yet. I have a plan for their asses.

Our tenth year wedding anniversary is in seven months. I can't help but to feel like we may not make it that far, but we have to in order for my plan to work. He wants to renew our vows, but for what? He doesn't take the vows we made to each other serious now, so what's the point? I'm going along with it though, especially since he has no knowledge that I know about his not so surreptitious love affairs. I know what he's been up to and it hurts. So bad! It's been so hard – faking like everything is all good.

The tears are beginning to fall rapidly as I sit here looking at the dozens of pictures that the private investigator I hired had dropped off to me. Not only did I have those in my possession, but also ones that I printed out at CVS on Centre Avenue from the chips to his phone.

There was a time when I wasn't suspicious of him at all and trusted him completely. That was until about six months ago, I started noticing different changes in the way he operated. Maurice is a 'routine' type of guy and things started changing drastically, causing my intuition to set off an alarm inside my soul. I knew something was up.

One day his phone was sitting on the island in the kitchen and it began ringing. I picked it up and saw it was his mother calling. I handed it to him over his shoulder while he had his feet kicked up on the coffee table watching the game. I hated when he put his dogs on my table! He missed the call by the time I handed it to him, but I was sure he'd be calling right back so I stood there. I watched as he drew the pattern to unlock his phone and call her back. I went to the bathroom to change the code on mine to match it so I wouldn't forget it.

Opportunity presented itself about a week later. He left his phone when he went to pick up our food. It was 'movie night' with the babies and we ordered some take out. My heart shattered into tiny little pieces when I entered the code in his phone. There were messages from women addressing him as Big Daddy, Babe, Bae – asking for sex, thanking him for sex, the whole nine. I went to his gallery and there was a plethora of pictures of various naked women in all kinds of positions – with and without clothes. I was utterly disgusted and beyond hurt. I managed to forward many of the pictures and messages to my own phone and then deleted any traces that I'd been in it at all. When he returned with our food, it was hard to contain the pain. He noticed a shift in my demeanor but said nothing. We all laid there watching Lion King for the umpteenth time, and then Shrek and Toy Story 3 before they finally knocked out. I went to bed right after without saying a word about what I'd found. I needed time to think and take it all in – and decide what I was going to do.

How could he do this to me? How could he do this to our family? What am I going to tell our babies, Micah and Milan... They are only six and four years old! Uuggh!! I let out a scream of frustration. I wanted to go out that door and kick some ass, but No, I got to play these cards just right. If it wasn't for my friend, who knows what these last six months would have been like. I've been getting some really great support and advice but the situation was getting all too real for me and I had some decisions to make.

I picked the photos up and tucked them away and decided to call my husband. His receptionist answered.

"Thank you for calling Dixon Real Estate and Architecture, what can we build for you today?'

I wanted to say, "A stronger foundation for my marriage," but of course I thought better of it. "Hi Xyla, this is MaKenzie. Is the Mr. there?"

"Oh, Hello Mrs. Dixon… Yes, he's in his office… putting you through right now. Hold the line please!"

I listened to a series of beeps and then he picked up.

"Hello Gorgeous, how's my beautiful wife?" …

Maurice

Technology is a mutha-fucka. I could see everything going on at my home, my offices, and my wife's shop from my phone with the push of a button. I'm sitting here in my office watching my wife have a break down. I couldn't see what was on them, but I saw that she had some pictures laid out across her desk. Whatever images those photos captured had her all fucked up – and had me shitting bricks at the same time. I'm a have to start paying closer attention to the cameras more often so I can find out what's going on with her.

She made me promise not to have cameras installed in her office because she didn't want to feel like someone was watching her all the time. She said it 'creeps her out'. She always said she only needed to know what was going on outside her door and would add that there was no point in her needing to "watch herself" work.

I tried to explain that it was for her safety and she always responded with, "Isn't that what the panic buttons in and around my office and several places around the shop are for? You and the police will be notified automatically if I or anyone else pushed one of them, so I'd be fine. And don't forget I'm licensed to carry. I'll bust a cap in someone's ass trying to come up in my place of business and mess with me."

I had to laugh just playing that back in my head with her prissy, yet think she's so tough ass.

That was one of many promises I've made but failed to keep. I'll be damned if I couldn't check up on her from wherever I was in or outside of the country.

What's bugging me is that she hasn't communicated to me that she was going through anything. This shit gots to be something internal going on with her, but what is it? If she knew I was fucking around on her *AND* had proof in the form of pictures, she would snap – which she hasn't done so I'm confused. *Why hasn't she talked to me about anything that's bothering her – unless it's me that's the issue?*

When we are together, shit is all good. Her beautiful smile is always present and bright – never looking forced and she treats me like her king – *always* -so I'm wondering - what the fuck is eating at my queen?

I know one thing, it bet not be no other man in her life that's for sure. I'll kill them both before I let some other muh-fucka take what's mine. This union is til' death do us…

Damn! Listen to me – got the most beautiful, intelligent, uber sexy, strong, successful wife and mother of my children and here I am a mutha-fuckin' dog. I've been fucking around with a few bitches, including one of her employees. Man, she would try to kill us both on sight if she ever found that shit out.

That's exactly why I told girly I wanted to get with her tonight. I planned on breaking it off – at least with her for right now, cause this shit is just wrong and too close to home, plus I can't shake the fact that I'm actually feeling her. I need to get out while I'm ahead before things get ugly. I'm bout nervous as shit, hoping she don't flip the script and wild out on me but fuck that – I'll body her ass before I let her fuck up my family.

MaKenzie, Micah, and Milan mean the world to me and I will stop at nothing to keep our family together. I done slipped up and fucked around and had sex with girly right in my wife's office and it things just got out of hand from there.

I was on a flight to attend a business meeting in Los Angeles, CA. that was to be held early the next morning. My company was one of three selected to bid on a structure that was to be built there. While on my way, I opened the security software on my phone. I decided to see what was going on at my wife's shop. It was a Monday and she was having a Welcome Party for one of the new girls she'd hired to be a nail tech. It looked like things were winding down. Carmen and Bella were leaving and everybody else left soon after. I had nothing else to do until I landed so I continued to watch. I remember thinking, "That chick Selena is looking right! She's pretty and her body is banging."

Lanel and the new girl were the last to leave. I saw them exchange words and then she headed to the Underground. I clicked the monitor to the Lounge and watched as girly poured herself another drink and then turned the music on. She started dancing, well gyrating and shit – feeling herself. I laughed, knowing she was tipsy. Nel came downstairs and I watched him watching her. Next thing you know, she was doing a dance on him which lead them to fucking in the corner booth in the back. I made a note to clear that scene from the tapes, but not before

making a copy for us to watch later on. That girl got moves!
She was entertaining to watch even with her clothes on.

*After the meeting, the shop was my first stop when I
returned to Pennsylvania so I could rap to my man Nel about his
lil deed. He's about to marry my wife's little sister. He tended
to work late so I swung by around ten, taking a chance on
whether he'd actually be there. He wasn't, but to my surprise,
Selena was. She was about to leave after doing her own hair as
I was coming in. We engaged in a small chat as she was
gathering her things. I was having a little trouble controlling
myself, watching her every move out the corner of my eye. She
bent down to pick up something and I looked directly at her ass.
She saw me and gave me a seductive smile as she slowly stood
up straight. "See something you like?" She asked and started
laughing. Instead of laughing shit off right with her, I said,
"Hell Yeah. And usually when I see something I like, I get it." I
grabbed my dick. I was a little surprised by her unexpected
answer. "Well come and get it Boo," she said as she licked
across her top lip. They were juicy as hell, covered in some type
of cherry looking gloss. She didn't have to tell me twice. Greg
was due in an hour and that was enough time to take it and go.
We fucked on the couch in MaKenzie's office and on top of her
desk.*

After that, it was on from there. The girl has some good
pussy and her head game is on point. She dropped to her knees
that very first night and I couldn't get enough. *This shit has to
stop!* I keep telling myself that but never seem to do it when I
get the chance. She takes me to another world, sexually, every
time I'm with her. I love smacking her on that fat ass she got
and the way she bends over for me to do it again every time.
The main problem with her is that trap of hers – she be getting
fly as shit and I be wanting to smack the taste out her mouth
sometimes.

The crazy part was that none of these bitches had shit on
my wife in *any* department in my eyes, yet every time I turned
around, I'm pulling out my dick for someone who was not her.

I'm about to drop all of these hoes though. Quite frankly, I'm tired of always trying to cover my tracks. That shit is tiresome and I'm getting too old for this shit. I have two separate chips for my phone - one to store my forbidden contacts and to hide all the naked pictures they send me. I mean ass shots, titty shots, pussy shots, whole body shots, videos of them pleasuring themselves – the whole nine; and then I have another for business, family, and for when I'm with my wife. I forgot my phone at home a while ago and was scared to go back up in there for fear she'd been in it. I hadn't changed the chip before going in and I was cursing myself the whole time I was gone. I noticed a shift in her mood when I got back but you know how women are. Mood swings left and right. Since I didn't get hit with a two-piece upon entry, I was relieved to have dodged that bullet, but this shit is getting old.

It's no secret that I am wealthy and hold a great amount of power in these streets. These bitches be laying the pussy at my feet before I even get a chance to know their name – hungry for the dick and the money and one thing they will never have the chance to get – my wife's position. That would never happen.

This shit with Selena happened on some humbug shit and unfortunately I fell in love with the pussy – not her – the pussy! It's just that good! I'm going to fuck her one last time tonight and then let her know we can't do this shit anymore. We'll see how that goes. I think she's falling hard for a nigga and I don't want to keep leading her on. I like her a lot, but I would never leave my wife for her and that's what she wants. *Not gonna happen*! I tell her what she wants to hear to appease her while making life easier for me, but that stops tonight because in reality – I'm only making shit worse.

My wife and I's tenth year wedding anniversary is in seven months and I've asked her to renew our vows. She agreed. I have been planning some very special surprises for her and I can't wait to make her the happiest woman alive – again. By the time our special day comes around, all these bitches and loose ends will be tied up. I'm turning in my player's card and giving my wife the love she deserves. Something I should have done a long time ago.

My thoughts were interrupted when my receptionist came through the speaker in my office, "Mr. Dixon, the Mrs. is on line one for you."

Speaking of my angel, here she is calling me now, "Hello Gorgeous, how's my beautiful wife?" …

Diagnosis: Complex Compatibility Syndrome

Nitra

So, here it is Tuesday. I've been missing in action from the Burgh for the last four days. After day one, I was supposed to be on my way home, never to say a word this man again, especially after he put his hands on me. But here I am, still here.

We have what you would call – "Complex Compatibility". Basically, no matter how hard we try, Jax and I can't seem to get enough of each other. There's just that much love between us. Our type of love should be forbidden. We are self-made soul mates with every reason in the book that we shouldn't be together, yet would never let each other go – at least completely, no matter how much we tried.

If you're wondering what happened to make me stay and choose to forgive him, let me tell you:

After our big fight Saturday morning, he left out of the house after I'd locked myself in his room and cried until I fell asleep. It was five o'clock in the evening when I finally woke up out of my depressed slumber. I'd slept for four and a half hours once my eyelids became too heavy to keep open and I eventually dozed off in the middle of my thoughts. More like fell into a temporary coma.

I knew Jax had come back home because the smell of the loud he was smoking hit my nose as soon as I opened my eyes. I contemplated giving him the silent treatment and keeping myself barricaded in his room for the rest of the night but the fact of the matter was I had to pee and I was hungry as hell. I probably lost ten pounds of water weight from all the damn tears I cried – for the second day in a row.

I opened the door and headed straight to the bathroom to relieve my bladder. It felt like I peed for five minutes straight. I got up, fixed my clothes and proceeded to wash my hands. I looked at myself in the mirror and instantly felt like shit because that is exactly what I felt I looked like – eyes all puffy and red, along with the rosy cheeks and a red nose. I splashed some cold water on my face a few times, brushed my teeth and did my best to fix my external appearance. My insides were so battered and bruised, my heart suffering the most trauma, that there was nothing I could do for the internal damage it incurred. When I finally got up the nerve to face the pain lurking outside the door, I took a deep breath and headed in that direction.

I couldn't believe my eyes when I stepped foot in the living room. It was filled with at least ten bags of clothes from various stores, five boxes of shoes, two purses and a vase full of pink and purple peonies – one of my favorite types of flowers.

"What's all this, I asked looking at all the merchandise sitting before me."

He looked up at me, letting some smoke blow out through his nose and said, "Yours. It's all yours. I'd give you the world if you'd allow me to. All I want is to be a part of it. I'm sorry for putting my hands on you and I promise that shit will never happen again. You were absolutely right when you said that was some bitch shit and I had to check myself. I was wrong – Dead Wrong. If you accept my apology, I promise I'll make it up to you. Whatever I have to do."

He stood up and walked towards me. I stepped back. He gave me that look like, "*Come on now.*" He held up a set of keys and dangled them in front of me, "These are for you too."

My eyes grew wide with shock and excitement. I knew instantly that those keys were to a car that he was telling me was mine. I didn't know what kind yet, but Lord knows I've been saving up for one for a long time and now I wouldn't have to buy one with my own money – meaning I now had five thousand dollars saved up that I could use for something else. I did my best to mask my excitement.

"So what, you think you can just buy your way out of this?" I asked with my arms crossed across my chest, not wanting to let him off so easy.

"Not at all… This is just *my* way of saying I'm sorry. If there's anything else I can do to fix this, I'll do it. So what is it? What I gotta do?"

He put on his best puppy dog face. The one that gets me every time!

He came closer and this time I stood still. He put his lips to mine and we embraced in one of those passionate kisses that never failed to make my body temperature rise. I almost fell under his spell but I was too anxious to see my new car.

Once again I forgot all about my appetite as I nudged him, "Well aren't you going to let me see my new toy?"

I asked him with a slight smile, still trying to hold on to somewhat of a grudge – not wanting to let him off the hook just yet. I had to see what he had out there. Shoot, it could be a 1990 Dodge Neon and that just wasn't going to cut it. I grabbed my keys out his hand and headed for the door. The suspense was killing me.

I let out a piercing scream as soon as I opened the door. I turned around and jumped up into his arms, wrapping my legs around his waist and my arms around his neck,

"Oh My God!" I said, giving him a kiss. "That's my car?" I asked, kissing him again.

He laughed at me, "Yup, that's *your* car. You like it?"

I unwrapped my legs from around his waist and stood on my tippy toes and kissed him again, "Like it? I fucking love it. Come on," I said, grabbing him by the arm, "Come let me take it for a spin."

He laughed at me again as I pulled him, forcing him into a light jog to get to it. I was too excited, unable to believe that my first car was a brand new 2012 champagne colored Mercedes C63 AMG Coupe. *Oh, I am going to be shitting on them back home.* I can't wait to show this off.

We got in the car and I started checking out the interior, pushing buttons, adjusting the mirrors and my seat. I fell in love instantly and I loved the new car smell. It was just right for me.

My stomach interrupted my celebration, reminding me that I hadn't eaten all day, so we decided to go get something to eat. Since I didn't know my way around, I decided I would let him drive – *this time*.

He ended up taking me to a spot called Double T Diner. My taste buds were set on breakfast and apparently his were too so that's what we ordered. We talked a little while we waited and I couldn't help but to think about ole girl and whether she knew I was staying with him and what exactly the status was between the two of them.

I asked him if he'd told Shakira I was staying a few days at his house. He took off his ball cap and sat it on the seat next to him and shifted a little in his position, passing his hand over his braids.

He leaned up with his elbows on the table and his hands folded, "Yea, she knows you're here. She doesn't know you're staying with me and it's really none of her business. I already told you we're just friends."

He said he told her I was his best friend and I came to visit him and to see how his lil cousin Terrance was doing now that he was making progress since he'd gotten shot. He told her we were having a bite to eat and she asked him to bring her something and to bring me with him so she could meet me.

"Are you okay with that?" he asked.

"Sure. I don't want her thinking I'm trying to take you off her hands or anything. I'm just visiting my *best friend* and his family right," I said sarcastically. "I promised you I'd visit soon didn't I – so here I am."

"Even though there was some level of force on your part, but I'm here nonetheless. And just because you bought me that car, I'm still here as your friend, nothing more, nothing less," I had to add.

He told me he was hoping to change that before I left.

After the waitress came with our food, it was so good that we basically ate in silence. I couldn't finish mine so I had the rest boxed up for later. He ordered chicky some breakfast to go and we talked some more while we waited and he told me more about the details surrounding the shooting. His little cousin now had a colostomy bag, but overall his condition was

109

improving dramatically. He was young and determined to bounce back stronger than he was before.

~~~~~~~~~

We pulled up to some row houses where Shakira lived. He turned off the engine, pulled out his phone and dialed her number to tell her we were outside. He got out and came to the other side and opened my door, letting me out of my ride he'd just bought me just hours ago. *A polite thug – how bout that*!

I felt funny about meeting her considering the history between us, but I was really only here as a friend as far as I was concerned. Jax can talk all that shit he wants about making me his woman, but I know him too well and can do without the bullshit that comes along with committing to him. This shit right here is just another one of his tests to see if I really mean what I say - wanting to see if I'm really going to pass up the possibility that the man of my dreams has been staring me in my face this whole time. *I think not*!

Yeah Right! - I know better. Jax is a ladies man and fine as hell at that. Shit, I'm sure Ms. Shakira isn't the only one, but she obviously mean something since he's *actually* introducing her to me.

I followed him to her door. He knocked twice and let himself in. We stepped into her home, entering the living room, which I noted was very clean and colorful. She came down a set of stairs that were to the left of the entrance and stepped right up to Jax, kissing him on the lips and taking the bag of food out of his hand.

"Thank you baby," she said as she stepped up, extending her hand, acknowledging that I was in her space. He

110

got right down to the introductions as I stood there feeling a twinge of jealousy creep up inside me.

"Shakira, this is my best friend Anitra. Nitra, Shakira."

We shook hands, both giving a fake smile, "Nice to meet you," I lied. "I hope you don't mind me coming to kick it with my boy for a couple days. Came to clear my head a little. Nice place you have here," I said looking around.

"Thank you, nice to meet you too," she lied back. She looked at Jax, "So what do you two have in mind to help her *clear her mind*."

She said that last part a little too slick in her tone for me.

"I know you want to show your friend a good time while she's here and I want to join in on the fun."

She kissed him on the lips again, I guess marking her territory some more. I took it as she was being smart. She knew what she was doing and rightfully so, but I didn't like her antics. I decided at that moment that I was going to show her who's boss. I'm the one who holds his heart and she only has him because I'm letting her.

I was going to let that be our little secret, between him and me, but since she want to play games – I decided to show her how it's played. I looked at Jax who saw the sparkle in my eye that said, "*It's On*." I just smiled and set my plan in motion.

"Yea Jax, what are we going to do to *clear my mind*? I say we all go to the club and have a few drinks and I can shake a lil tail feather on the dance floor." I did a lil booty shake, letting out a giggle and turning to Shakira, "What do you say? Where's a nice spot to go to around here? Where are all the fine, sexy, single men at in this town?"

111

I noticed Jax give me a look like he just smelled a ton of bullshit on my breath that smacked him square in his nostrils. Of course she didn't notice the look he gave me, too busy jumping at the invitation to tag along thinking she blocking something. We decided to meet up at a club she suggested and it was on from there.

As soon as we got back in the car he says, "Aye Nitra, don't be fucking playing with me like that. That's that bullshit you just pulled. But you know what, we going go out tonight and you bet not be up in no other man's face – especially not in my presence. Period. Don't make me body a nigga in front of crowd full of people. That's not my style, but I'll do it. You trying to be funny cause girly was in there kissing on me ain't you? Do I sense a bit of jealousy coming from you?"

I looked at him and laughed in his face as I put my seatbelt on. "Oh, so you're threatening me again now? Don't flatter yourself. I already told you I want nothing but friendship from you. She can have you and the rest of the headaches that come along with being your woman."

He started the engine, giving me his mean mug. The one I found to be so sexy on him. I guess I just have a thing for bad guys.

"What is that supposed to mean? Man, fuck that friendship shit you keep talking. You know what it is. And you sure snapped out of your headache when you seen this mutha fuckin' car."

He struck a nerve, reminding me that I had a headache earlier and that he, in fact, was the reason I had it, and the reason I forgot all about it in an instant at the same damn time. I whispered in my head, "*Asshole.*" He gets on my last nerve! *Uugh*!!

112

I got that disgusted scowl on my face and stated matter-of-factly, "Don't even go there. And if you think because you bought me this car it means you can run my life - you can take this bitch back. I don't remember saying I was your woman *before* you bought the damn car, and haven't a damn thing changed *after*. You said it was your way of saying you were sorry. Me keeping it is my way of accepting your apology. You don't get to throw it up in my face anymore, okay?"

I was clearly pissed and he could hear it in my tone. Not wanting to takes ten steps backwards, he let it go for now and moved on. I was taking advantage of his earlier transgressions and using it to my benefit. On a regular day, he never paused at checking me when he felt my mouth was getting too fly.

The Showdown

Later that night....

The club had to be filled to capacity. People lined the place from wall to wall and the dance floor was all the way live. Shakira decided she'd meet us there because she was still getting dressed by the time we were ready. I guess she had to make sure she was on point because she damn sure knew I would be.

She was the one in competition. As far as I was concerned, I already won the race. The fact that she's not me was disqualification enough in his eyes, so she should be thanking me for not wanting his ass.

By the time she got there, we'd already had three shots of Patron between the two of us, and was on our second bottle of Ace of Spades. I was feeling real nice. Too nice actually.

"There's your girlfriend," I said to him when I noticed Ms. Thing making her way to the V.I.P section where we were chilling at, people watching and the likes.

She walked straight up to him, putting her arms around his neck and once again, kissed him on the lips just as she had done earlier. Her eyes were closed and he was looking at me. I shook my head and turned away from them, making my way to the dance floor.

"Ain't nobody fucking with my clique" was playing through the speaker. I danced in place by myself until the song went off. The next jam faded in and I started doing what the lyrics was telling me to do, which was, "Drop it low girl, drop it drop it low girl...."

I knew Jax's eyes would be glued to me – especially now that some cutie with a bald head and neatly trimmed facial hair walked up on me, all up in my space. I looked in their direction and just like I said, he was watching me – while she watched him watching me. He keep talking all that wanting me to be his woman shit and letting another woman kiss all over him in my presence. *Fuck all that*! I had something for both of they asses. It was *my* turn to get up under both of their skin. I turned the heat up in that bitch.

For the next four songs, I showed them how Pittsburgh girls get down up in there. I was doing my dance so well, I now had an audience and people crowding around me cheering me on. The same sexy, bald head guy with the straw hanging out his mouth was still pushing up on me, holding my waist as I broke it down. By the time the last song was over, I was tired and sweating. I thanked the gentleman for the dance and sashayed away, knowing he'd be right behind me. He followed me off the dance floor over to the bar just like I knew he would.

"Can I buy you a drink," he asked. He extended his hand and I gave him mine. "I'm Zo, and you are?" He raised my hand, bringing it to his lips and placed a soft kiss on the back of it.

"Anitra. And I'll have a shot of Patron, thanks." He waved the bartender down and ordered us both a shot.

He raised his glass, "Let's toast…. To Beautiful Ladies."

I smiled a seductive grin, raising my glass to meet his, "To Handsome Men who know a beautiful lady when he sees one." We threw them back.

We started making small talk about where I was from and such. You know I had to make it known that I was from none other than Sixburgh, Pennsylvania. Repping my Steelers in Ravens town.

Black & Yellow All Day!!

"They say Pittsburgh has the biggest women fan base. I see you're part of the crowd." His voice was very robust and sexy.

I showed him my tattoo of the three diamonds from the Steelers emblem behind my ear, but closer to my neck. He acted like he needed a closer look and placed a soft kiss on my artwork.

"I don't mind playing in enemy territory," he joked. His voice was mesmerizing. He complimented me some more. "You have some pretty lips. Can I kiss them?"

I was so caught up in his gaze, the touch of his hand on my chin, and his fragrance tickling my nose that I actually leaned in to allow him to kiss me.

116

Before our lips got the chance to touch, I was being snatched by the arm, "What the fuck are you doing Nitra? Bout to kiss some random ass nigga. You don't even know this cat. You drunk as hell," Jax barked, with Shakira standing at his side.

She had a disgusted look on her face.

Zo put his hands up in the surrender position, "Whoa now. Is this your girl?"

Jax mean mugged the shit out of him, "No, she ain't my girl but she still off limits dog."

No was all Zo needed to hear. He stepped forward, standing man to man with Jax and said, "How so? If she's not your girl then what the fuck is your issue? She look like a grown ass woman to me."

I guess he thought about it quickly and didn't want any further drama or confrontation to occur so he said, "You know what,?" he paused, pulled out his wallet and retrieved a business card. He put it in my hand and said, "Call me when you're free," and walked away.

Jax grabbed me by my waist, pulling me away from the bar area towards the exit, "It's time to go. Your ass is drunk and bout to have me kill a muh-fucka in here."

Kira chimed in, "And why is that Jax? You jealous? The girl is single and like he said, she's grown. Let her have some fun."

I agreed with the wench in that moment.

"Yea, Jax, I'm *Sin-gle*, let me have some fun," I mocked her while adding a draw to the word single. He told me to shut up and that he was taking me to my hotel room.

This jerk had just told a bold faced lie right in my face. I was drunk, but wasn't nothing slow about me. He still didn't want her to know I was staying at his house.

I am woman – and women know other women… and I knew she didn't believe him. I was sure she was going to stop by to make sure he was sleeping in his bed – alone.

I knew what it was hitting for as soon as we got to his house. Since the whole incident was all part of my plan to show both these mugs who was boss, I was already prepared to control the whole situation.

He started talking shit as he was getting out of the car, thinking I was going to join in on a screaming match with him, but I had something else in mind.

I didn't even trip about him choosing to park my car in his garage instead of right out front next to his where it's been. He wanted her to think I wasn't in there just in case she decided to stop by. We stepped in the house and he made sure to lock the door behind him. I headed straight to the bathroom and got undressed. I came out butt naked and stood in the doorway to his bedroom where he'd taken a seat on the bed. He looked up at me ready to talk some more shit but was blind-sided by my goods staring him in the face.

"Can't you just be a lover and *not* a fighter for the rest of tonight," I asked him.

I knew I had him right where I wanted him since I knew he thought he wasn't getting any sex from me because of the fight we had earlier.

"Say no more," he responded.

I told him to take his clothes off and lay back while I went to get some whipped cream out of the refrigerator.

I made sure to unlock the door so girly could walk right in. I knew she was coming. I would have come to check up on that ass too, especially with a woman as fine as me lurking around his sexy self.

I did my thing with the whip cream, setting his desires on fire. I did what I've only done to him and sucked the shit out of his dick. That surprised him because I really didn't like to do it and he knew that. Next thing you know we were sparring between them sheets.

By the third round, your girl didn't disappoint. She showed up while he was knee deep in the pussy, telling me how much he loved me as he collapsed on top of me. She stood there watching for at least ten minutes. I acted like I was just as shocked as he was when she finally spoke up.

"What the fuck Jax?" she screamed.

He jumped, grabbing the covers, pulling them over our naked bodies, "What the fuck? How did you get in here?"

He looked at me, then back at her with eyebrows so tight they almost became one. She started crying and ran out the bedroom door, down the hall, making an exit out his front door. He didn't even chase after her. *That had to hurt.*

He let out one of those "*what the fuck... this shit is crazy*" laughs. I pulled the covers up to my neck and turned on my side, thinking, "*Good for the both of them!*"

My plan worked like a charm. I slept good that night. She most definitely didn't. And once I went back home, he wasn't going to either.

~~~~~~

The last couple of days have been Shakira free. I take it she's done with him. He's cool though. He'll be on to the next as soon as I'm gone.

We were sitting at the island in the kitchen eating lunch and his phone rang. Whoever it was on the other end, I could tell something was wrong by the look on his face.

"Okay, okay, we're on our way." He ended the call, "We got to go baby. Your grandma is being rushed to the hospital." I instantly felt dizzy.

"What? What's wrong Jax? What happened? Is she okay? Who was that?" I started hitting him with question after question, not giving him a chance to respond to any of them.

"Calm down baby girl. She was having chest pains and called my mom. My mom called the paramedics and she's following them to the hospital now."

120

He finally gave me my phone back. I was avoiding talking to anyone but my grandmother – really using this time away to clear my head. Now it's back to reality I go. *Play times over.*

We gathered up my things. He bought me so much in the few days I've been down here that there wasn't room for anything else to fit in my car.

I followed him all the way home. We never stopped until we pulled up at Mercy Hospital's Emergency Department where my grandmother was being treated after suffering what we believed was a heart attack. I vowed I wasn't ever leaving her again. I don't know what I would have done if we drove for hours to find my grandma dead instead of alive.

Fear Factor

When we got to the hospital, I rushed to the emergency station to speak with someone about my grandmother's condition. The woman at the desk checked the system, informing me that she had been admitted and had already been escorted to a regular room. Once we made our way to the floor where they monitor heart patients, we stepped in her room quietly to find her hooked up to monitors with a tube in her nose pumping continuous oxygen and her arm hooked to an I.V., resting peacefully in the Clinitron hospital bed.

I stood at one side and kissed her on the cheek while Jax stood on the other, placing a kiss on her forehead. Looking down at her, I felt so bad for staying away for all these days, knowing how sick she's been lately and instantly started feeling guilty. I looked up at Jax, feeling a little resentment towards him for insisting I go.

"I told you I didn't want to leave her," I said, looking back down at her with eyes full of tears.

He came over to where I was standing and placed both hands on my shoulders as he turned me to face him. He used his thumbs to wipe my tears.

"I'm sorry baby. I only insisted because I was going crazy not seeing you and you were avoiding me and not answering my calls or responding to my messages. I needed to see you. I just wanted to spend some time with you and now that I had the chance, I'm good. That is if we're good. Are we good?" He asked with concern in his eyes, pulling me close to him and holding me tight.

I missed my chance to speak as he capitalized on my pause and continued, "You know Ms. Lorene is my heart too. I'm glad it wasn't the worst that could happen which is her leaving here, but of course this my feisty little lady right here," he said turning me loose and looking down at my gram, placing his hands on the rail of her bed. "She's a fighter... She's tough... and she's not leaving until she at least gets the chance to see her great grandchildren she's waiting for us to have."

He looked at me and my face did some sort of contorted transformation, ending up at stuck-on-stupid and we both had to laugh.

"I don't think so Buddy," I told him, laughing as I saw my gram open her eyes and smile.

"Hey grandma! I'm so happy you're okay. I'm not leaving you ever again," I told her, leaning in to kiss her cheek again, wiping my eyes at the same time.

"How else you going to make them babies?" she had the nerve to say. We all laughed a little.

Jax made sure to compound on the moment some more saying, "She still refusing to be my wife Ms. Lorene. Can you believe that?" *Like he was telling on somebody.* "I keep telling her we need to quit playing so you can meet our babies, but don't worry, I'm going to keep working on her and maybe she'll finally want to start our family someday soon. I Love Her." He looked up at me, "I Love You!"

He was trying to use my grandma's love for him to his advantage but I wasn't going to let him.

"Whatever Jax! I'll deal with you later but right now I need to talk to a doctor about what's going on with my grandma.

I'll call you later, but right now, I could actually use some time alone with her, please."

I was totally unwilling to go through the motions with him any longer, and definitely not right now. I'm more concerned about my gram and her health than me and him and I damn sure don't want to talk about commitment, let alone some damn babies, and especially with him.

I really did appreciate him buying me the car, but I honestly wasn't sure I would ever feel the same about him again after what he'd done. That hurt me to the core. I saw something in him this weekend that I'd never seen before and it scared me. I know he's a walking threat to society, but I've never felt like he was a threat to me – until now. We have, well had, something so special. It's like he's the Hulk and I'm the only girl, the only person who could calm him and bring him back down to size. He treated me with such delicacy because of that.

To me, it's like ever since I mentioned wanting to see someone else and possibly pursue a relationship with someone other than him, he changed. And once he saw that I had an attraction to Haj, on top of me admitting I had sex with him, it must have sent him over the edge.

But fuck that, he had Lil Ms. Thing in his life. So what am I supposed to do? I love Jax, but I don't want to be with him. I can't - and I was just about to tell him that when his mother walked in the room.

"Hey yall!. How long yall been here? I ran to get something to eat right quick while Ms. Lorene was sleeping." She came over to me and gave me a fake ass hug. "I knew yall were on yall's way. Yall got here fast."

124

She continued, "Hey Son, it's always good to see you. " She turned and looked me up and down and went on, "And look at you. You glowing girl, with your pretty self."

She was very animated, as usual. She probably would have pinched my cheeks if she thought she'd get away with it. *She know better!*

"How long yall been here?" She repeated the question that she didn't give us the chance to answer the first time.

Jax answered her, "We just got here about fifteen minutes ago."

She then walked over and gave her son a hug, noticing my grandmother was awake.

"Hey Ms. Lorene. You're up! Look who's here!" She stated the obvious.

Ms. Joyce doesn't care for me that much, and she know it. I knew it and Jax knew it. Even though she never acted as such in front of my grandma or anyone else for that matter, there was no doubt about it. She would tell Jax that I thought I was too good for him and that he should stop chasing behind my little stuck up ass. That's what he told me she said, among other things, and ever since then, I kept things real short with her.

I always picked up on her attitude when I was around and her little snide, sarcastic remarks, but I didn't want to disrespect her on the strength of him. I never bothered telling my grandma how fake she was because I truly did not care what she thought of me. Shoo, I have some thoughts of my own about her. Yes, she moved her son out of Pittsburgh because she didn't want him to get killed, but the truth of the matter is, she supported his lifestyle simply because she felt it helped to upgrade hers. She didn't care what kind of havoc he was reeking out here on these streets for the last several years. She only cares that *he* didn't get hurt, or worse, killed in the process.

Sure I talked bad to him and wasn't willing to risk my life for no amount of money or material gain. I know the life he chose for himself and I am not signing my own death certificate by committing myself to a man whose blood it'd be written in. It would only be a matter of time before he's dead or in jail and when the time comes, I don't want to be anywhere around, because I'm sure it will be ugly. He made that clear on several occasions.

"I'm not going out without a fight. Shit, I'm going out with a bang, cause ya know whenever they decide to come after me, I'm going to have my gun in hand. Them muh-fuckas gon' have to kill me. I'll be damn if I go willingly to the cage," he would say.

One would wonder how I could be involved with a man such as Jax … And all I can say is that we grew up together and have shared so much with each other, experiencing life and things with one another. I know a side of him that no one else gets to see – his softer side. Unfortunately – "His softer side may last through the night, but the Thug in him rises in the morning."

Jax and Ms. Joyce stayed for about another half an hour and finally said their goodbyes. My grandma had already dozed off again, so I decided I'd at least walk him to his car.

He told me his vibe wasn't right and that he didn't think it was a good idea for him to stay in town right now. I understood. He was hitting the road as soon as he left the hospital and we laughed - he knew he was in for an ear beating because he hadn't told his mom he wasn't staying.

126

Of course we shared a kiss. I told him to call me when
he got back so I know he made it safely, as I always did. I
almost wanted to tell him to make a way to come back and get
the car. I felt bad for keeping it knowing I could never be with
him the way he wanted me to, but then I said to myself, "Nah,
you deserve this car Nitra. He hurt you and it's his way of
saying he's sorry. That's what he said." I of course agreed with
myself and dismissed the thought of giving it back immediately.
I was keeping the damn car and wasn't kidding anyone but
myself that it would be otherwise.

I turned and headed back inside the hospital. I usually
watched him until he was out of sight, but this time I couldn't. I
had to get him out of my mind and out of my heart - Starting
now.

I returned to my grandmother's room and two doctors
were in there and she was awake *again*.

The short one with the glasses extended his hand, "You
must be Anitra. Nice to meet you."

She must have told them I was in the building.

"Yes, I'm Anitra," I replied, giving them both a smile
and a nod as I shook his hand. The taller one removed his hands
from his pockets and shook my hand as well. He was fly let me
tell you. He was young, Asian, handsome, and a doctor –
Mmmm, and he looked good enough to eat. My hot girl inside
stood up and started checking him out with one hand on her hip,
neck cocked to the side and her other hand at the brim of her
brow like she was saying "Salute!" I chuckled at her. *"Sit your
lil hot ass down!"*

My thoughts shifted immediately. Haji was on my mind
strong and I'd been thinking about him this whole time, wanting

to call him. I even dialed his number and pressed Talk, only to press End to terminate the call before his phone had a chance to ring. I'm going to call him soon, but I really don't know what I'm going to say, what I want to say – where do I begin?

I just stayed away from him, fleeing to another state, with another man and not to mention had sex with both of them within a day apart. *That was stupid!* A drunk ain't shit! Once again I'm blaming it on the alcohol. And the fact that Jax wasn't going to take no for an answer and I was going rather I wanted to or not.

I know he's not going to be trying to hear that, so for now, when I do talk to him, I plan to be honest, but of course I am also going to just to omit that part. He doesn't need to know that and let's not forget, he has a fucking wife, separated or not. *That bitch is already a problem!*

The thing that happened with Jax and I was just a silly game of me showing the lil sarcastic, call-herself-being-smart broad who was boss – and I won – I'm the Queen, numero uno in Jayson Calloway's heart.

"She'ont Know Nann? If she didn't, then she does now." I had to laugh at myself on that thought.

If I want to be with Haji, I need to get it together, but I've already decided that would not happen until he was actually divorced. And Jax - he is done, I'm moving on and he's just going to have to get over it and let me go.

I turned my attention back to the doctors.

"Nice to meet you gentleman as well. How's my lady doing doc?"

I looked at my grandmother laying in that bed and came to the conclusion that she hadn't been able to get any real rest, at least not since I arrived at the hospital. She looked weak, and her eyes looked weary to me, like she really needed some sleep.

The doctors explained what was going on with her and their plans for treatment. She has an infection in her lungs that they are treating with I.V. antibiotics and she had also suffered a mild heart attack. She will be undergoing some additional testing while she's here and they estimated that she would be here at least a week. They assured us she was in good hands and promised they'd take good care of her and even added that for the most part, she was actually rather healthy for a woman her age.

After they left, I urged her to sleep and told her I was going home to unload my stuff from my new car. I smiled at the thought of having my own *fly* ride outside and not needing to call anyone or catch the bus or a cab.

She admitted she felt worn out and was going to sleep until I returned. I made sure to stop at the nurse's station to tell her nurse, Sheila, to call me if any visitors came while I was gone because she really needed to rest. She was so nice and accommodating and she agreed to my request.

The last thing I want is my mother's ass coming up in here bothering every-damn-body on the floor – having no respect for the fact that it's a damn hospital, with sick people, who needed their rest – and that included my gram. I can just see her now - acting all loud and ghetto. Asking dumb ass questions, getting on people's nerves...

Just the thought of her popping up while I was gone gave me a slight headache.

On the ride home, I decided it was a good idea to call MaKenzie and let her know I was home and would be returning to work in the morning. She was very happy to hear from me at first and then the conversation turned a little serious.

She was concerned, worried that something was wrong and also felt I should have called sooner because it was the considerate thing to do. I apologized ten times and told her I'd give her all the details when I came in.

She told me about her talk with Haj and how he'd been checking up on my grandma and missing me. I smiled. My heart smiled. "He is so considerate," I thought, wishing things were different with his situation.

MaKenzie made it a point to tell me a little about heartbreak and hurt feelings and how she understood why I was upset. I heard sincerity and even sensed a hint of pain in her voice as she expressed her thoughts on the situation based on the conversation she had with him. Even though she hadn't heard my side of the story, nor did we get into what he had actually said to her, she felt I overreacted and should have given the man a chance to explain. I, on the other hand, was totally surprised at her position considering he's married and so is she. You'd think she would be totally against that kind of arrangement and trying to talk me out of it, but instead, what I was getting from her was encouragement.

"For what it's worth, I think you should forgive him."

Without explaining or going into detail about why she felt that way, she stressed her point, which was that she felt he was deserving of a chance.

HOW? – He's freaking *MARRIED*!!!

"Over the past several days, I've had time to think about everything and you know what, you're right. The least I could do is talk to him. Yes, I can forgive him for not telling me right away, but I don't think I can be with him MaKenzie. He has a wife and separated or not, I'd rather he were divorced before we did anything more. I had sex with him Kenzie and I feel stupid because there is another woman, a wife – in his life. And she's pregnant. Did he tell you that? This situation got me all confused because I really started catching feelings for him, you know? He's all I thought about while I was gone."

I took a breath, paused for a moment and then continued without interruption from MaKenzie, "Oh, and Jax, he pretty much blew it...And then he goes out and buys me a car to try to make up for it. But I don't think things will ever be the same. Wait 'til I tell you," I told her as I was about to swing the bend and pull up at my house.

"What? He bought you a car? What the fuck did he do to you Nitra? Had to be something crazy if a nigga buying cars to say sorry and shit!"

I laughed.

"Yes, it was crazy. That's why I'm going to need to tell you in person. Let's just say he snapped. He snapped and came back with a 2012 C63 AMG Coupe for my ass. He knew I'd been saving up for a car and figured I'd definitely accept his apology once I saw it. He was right. I love this car!"

At first there was silence. If I know MaKenzie, she was picking her mouth up off the floor.

"WHAT? Wait... Hol'up... What you mean he snapped? What he do Nitra? He hit you didn't he? Why else would he take such drastic measures to say sorry? Mm, Mm,

Mm…Haj is going to trip when you tell him about this shit Nitra, and how the hell you gonna explain the car? No, no, no! I don't care what kind of car it is. You can't be letting anyone put their hands on you and then think they can buy you something to make it okay."

She was feeling some type of way. I honestly hadn't thought about how Haji was going to feel once he saw me driving this car.

At the same time, I was thinking, "*Is she not hearing me?*" I mean, I care about his feelings, but not enough to excuse the fact that he has a whole 'nother life with somebody else that isn't officially over and on top of that – she's pregnant. I wasn't about to give too much of a fuck about his feelings in the first place due to that fact alone.

"Awe man. You know I hadn't thought about how Haji would feel. I was so happy that I had a new car, and a fly one at that, and would be able to use the money I've been saving on other things I needed, that it never crossed my mind. Oh My God, what should I say? What should I do? Why is my heart all twisted up in a knot about this? I shouldn't care what he would say or think, but the truth is I do." *Just said I wasn't gon' care too much about his feelings – Not going well…*

I started to panic. I made up my mind that I wanted to be with him and not Jax, but how the hell do I tell him…

"*Um, yea, Baby – I'm ready to make it official. I did just come from staying four days with Jax and he bought me a car and we had sex, but only because his bitch was being smart, but that's over and I really want to be with you – and keep the car he bought me. BUT you have to get rid of her before we do anything.*"

132

He's not going for that. Huuughhh!!! It was time for me to end this call. I needed time to think. I apologized one more time to my wonderful boss and promised to get better where communication is concerned. She of course reiterated how much she adored me and how I am like a little sister to her. I appreciated having someone mature to talk to and how she always keeps it real with me.

"To answer your question, I'd say you listen to your heart, tell him the truth and take it from there. And one more thing - when you do finally talk to him, Listen! From the stuff he had to say about him and ole girl's situation – I'd be surprised if she ain't up to something."

"Okay, thanks Kenzie. I really appreciate you, I really do. But, let me get off here and get this stuff in the house. See you tomorrow."

"See you tomorrow Hun."

We hung up and once again I instantly thought about calling Haj. Only problem is every time I went to call, I got butterflies in my stomach and I wasn't exactly sure why. I didn't know if I was nervous? Scared…of his reaction? Ashamed? Confused? Undecided? - I don't know, but whatever it was got the best of me as I decided against calling him just yet – Again.

Still Wifey, For Now...

Michelle

I'm not in love with Haji and when I really think about it, I never was. I was with him simply because it was convenient and beneficial for me. Don't get me wrong – I do have feelings for him, but I've always been in love with money and that's truly all I was concerned with. *Sad, but true*!

He is such a man's man. He's a provider, protector and *sexy as hell*. The gym in the basement does his body good. He's not big on being buff, just fit. He is a sight for sore eyes as they say! A different picture of him for every month of the year on a calendar that hung on your wall in your bedroom would totally turn you on.

He's quite the militant and that's what people really don't know about him and also what I found to be his sexiest trait. He's a bad boy with amazing self-control. He reads a lot. Books like "The Art of War", "The Art of Deception", and "Behold a Pale Horse."

Shit that fed his mind, as he says. Tired of settling for an existence subpar to who he really was is how he explained it.

He is…versatile and volatile and more importantly, a Thinker – and with him, it's definitely a lethal combination of qualities to possess. He's very intelligent, calculating, and have I said …handsome.

Might I add – *Rich*!

And that, my friend, was the only thing I cared about – The Money. Well, the dick too, cause that man can make a bitch cry every time, but the rest of the shit I could give two fucks about – especially love. That shit is overrated! A man gon' be a man and before I let a man crush my heart, I decided a long time ago that I was going to be a Bitch – and a bad bitch while I'm at it – ready to play the game with these niggas and beat them at their own shit.

I was prepared to keep my heart under lock and key. I threw that bitch in the river a long time ago so no man will ever have my heart again. The first and only mother fucker to get it, destroyed it. He definitely fucked it up for even the best of them – I figured they are all the fucking same, including Haj, and therefore I have no love for any of these fools.

For the average bitch, he's the perfect man. But that's just it – I'm not your average bitch.

To be honest, I was surprised a broad such as myself even got him to wife me in the first place. The truth of the matter is I knew all along that he didn't marry me because he loved me, but only because I was carrying his seed.

I was only marrying him for the money anyway, so I didn't give a fuck. If anything were to happen, I was getting *Half*!

I would be lying if I didn't say that, at times, I wondered what it would be like right now had our son lived. He was so determined to give his child a family and a life he deserved, that he stopped hustling and all of his other ill methods of making money. And he made money. Lots of it, and fast.

He ended up tying the knot with me when I was six months pregnant. He started a legit business, Preferred Professionals Cleaning Co. I helped him come up with the name and was one of the first workers on his payroll. I still work for him, but I wasn't sure how long that was going to last. He's been seeing some lil young bitch and I'm sure once she finds out I work for him, she's going to try to talk him into cutting ties with me out of insecurity. I tend to have that effect on every bitch he called himself doing something with – just fucking or otherwise, and as you see, none of them prevailed. I'm still his wife, even if we've been separated for over a year... and where are them bitches at? – *Gone!*

He can't get enough of this pussy and head game if he wanted to. I know what he likes and have no problem doing it – especially when I want something. In this case, I can see he has feelings for this hoe, especially since she answering his phone and shit. He's never done that bullshit before so shit must be getting serious. For right now I had nothing to worry about though. As long as he thinks I'm pregnant, he won't be going anywhere – at least not too far.

After he started the business, he started working and reading heavy. He evolved into an intelligent thug as I liked to call him. He was smart and all that but the man is still crazy. Don't let the calm, cool, and collective demeanor fool you. I am and have always been hood so the shit doesn't scare me. It actually turns me on.

Those who *know* me, call me The Devil in Drag. I've heard it said that I'm just an evil bitch who only cares about one thing, and that's getting money. *Bingo!* – *Right On!* *If it don't make dollars, it don't make sense.*

Haji was getting major dollars and I had sense enough to stick around so I could secure his money as my own. That's exactly what brought him and I together in the first place – money....

I worked for his boy, Vaughn, a hustler and stick-up man from the North Side…me and some other chick named Kamryn. I didn't like the broad at first. She had this vibe about her that rubbed me the wrong way. He sensed the tension and told us to get to know each other because we'd be working together whether we liked it or not. He didn't need nor want any catty women who couldn't get along, hating on each other on his team.

Kam would get a hotel room in her name every weekend and Vaughn would meet us there at ten p.m. every Friday and Saturday, sometimes switching it up, calling himself giving us the element of surprise, showing up almost an hour or two late, and sometimes early. He didn't want us having any "company" while we were handling business for him either. He'd kill someone if he found out they knew anything about his operation and that was no bullshit. The mistake was made only once and he saw to it that we knew better when it came to disobeying his orders. He offed this dude right in front of us. I always said his blood was on Kam's hands since she was the one who told him to come smoke some green with us in the first place.

We had different jobs to do – the main one being counting money. *Ain't that some shit.* Nigga had so much money, he paid us to count it, band it up and pack it neatly in black briefcases. Boy did I love my job. He's the reason I can't get enough. It was because of him that so much paper has gone through these pretty manicured hands of mine and I needed it in my life. I didn't mind getting my hands dirty when it came to the dough.

One weekend, he came to the room with Haj with him and that's when it all began. I figured they must have been really close because he never brought anyone with him. He does everything alone.

137

Vaughn and Haj sat on the couch smoking while we did our thing at the counter in the kitchen area. This time we counted money, plus they brought two pounds of weed and asked us to bag it up, giving both of us a scale. It took us two hours to bust that shit down. After we were finished, we joined in on their two man party. We took shots and smoked a good four blunts of loud, back to back, and one thing led to another. We were all highed up and tipsy and to this day I believe Vaughn's simple ass put some ecstasy in our drinks. His friend seemed more laid back than him. Vaughn is a fucking wild fire – do and say anything to anybody, anywhere type of nigga – which was exactly why I didn't put shit past him.

He ended up fucking Kam on the couch, while I fucked Haj on the bed. That's actually all it took. We didn't use protection and I put it on him so good that he couldn't pull out. I normally would take the morning after pill just to be on the safe side, but I figured if he was with Vaughn, he had to be rolling in some major dough and a baby would be all I needed to get him to come up off some of it. It would be my ticket to some continuous cash flow.

When I first told him I was pregnant, it was over the phone and he hung up on me. I didn't hear from him for two weeks after my initial phone call. I didn't give a fuck and wasn't going to keep it anyway, so I didn't trip and start acting simple like only I knew how. Instead, I made an appointment to have an abortion and called it a day.

He, on the other hand, looked at my lack of drama in the form of text, curse-word-laced voicemails or any other form of harassment as a sign of my maturity. *Sucker*! He ended up calling to apologize. We talked and I decided to play him close – he had money and the dick was fire and I wanted to keep him around. I started playing my part. I fucked him good and

138

sucked him better. I threw down in the kitchen and kept his house clean, being quite the homemaker while he handled his business.

He was being very attentive to my belly, talking to it, rubbing it and singing songs to it. The baby would respond to his voice and the music by bumping around and kicking like crazy every time. For a minute, I thought I was going to fall in love. By the time I was six months, we were down at the justice of the peace, exchanging vows. I guess you could call it one of the best days of both our lives since he was giving his son a family and I was now married to the money. At that moment, I felt like I had him right where I wanted him. Even if we didn't last, I didn't sign a pre-nup, so half his shit would be mine. Shit, he didn't even have to go this far – I would have been cool just being his baby mama, but this made things even sweeter – it secured payments to my bank account for at least the next eighteen years. With the money he has, I would be sitting pretty with or without him.

About a month after we were married, I started showing my true colors. I truly didn't care whether we worked out or not. I figured I'd just sue him for alimony and get my money anyway. One night, things totally went left all over a glass of damn liquor....

He had come home one evening after work. I made dinner and called myself setting the mood with candles and wine and some soft, sultry music. All was going well until I filled two glasses with Hennessy, his drink of choice, instead of one.

"Both of them are for me, right?" he asked me with a straight face.

"Hell naw, we going to enjoy all of this together," I said, with me and my big belly trying to straddle his lap. I was

waving my hand around, reminding him of the ambiance I had
going on in the room. He stopped me and stood up.

"You can't be serious right now… Matter of fact, you
can't be that stupid. You think I'm going to sit here and drink
with you while you're carrying my baby. I'm trying to do the
right thing Chelle, but you're not making this easy. At first you
seemed like you at least had some common sense about you, but
lately I've been seeing, not so much. I'm going to say this one
time and one time only. I don't give a fuck what you do after you
have this baby, but you better act like you got some damn sense
until then. You keep on with the bullshit… if something comes
up wrong with my son… I'm taking him off you and I'm not
fucking with your ass."

I knew he was serious. I saw the fire in his eyes right
before he grabbed his keys and left. I ended up drinking both
our glasses of Henny and damn near finished the rest of the
bottle. He didn't come home that night.

He stopped coming home every night and his whole
attitude towards me changed from that day forward. I continued
drinking heavy, popping pills and all kinds of shit up under the
sun that you shouldn't do while pregnant. The baby was alive
every time I went to my appointments so I didn't think anything
of it.

Come my due date, I went to the hospital to have a baby
only for it to be stillborn. I was happy as hell but Haj was hurt,
angry and upset. He really shut me out after that. He would
only come home to shit, shave and shower. He didn't even eat at
home. I grew tired of his bullshit and started doing my own
thing without caring what he thought or felt, or caring what
happened to the got damn baby.

Now, he thinks I'm pregnant again since I sent him that pic of Kam's little sister's pregnancy test. That is the only thing that will make him soften his heart towards me and start coming up off more money than what he's giving me to work for him. He may even come back to me if I show him "*I've changed*". I can tell he is really starting to catch feelings for this new bitch and I'll be damned if he thinks he's going to move on and give her everything and leave me stuck. He got another thing coming – It will be over my dead body, or hers.

For now, I just need to get him over here and entice him into having sex with me, hoping he *really* gets me pregnant in the process. My plan will fail if he doesn't, but again, I know what he likes, and how he likes it, so I don't intend to do anything but win. *I'm calling his ass right now*! Time to set the plan in full swing.

But You're Perfect For Me

Nitra

I went back to the hospital to sit with my gram at least until visiting hours were over. I got upstairs to her room and as I walked in, my heart shot right to the floor. My grandmother was still resting peacefully and was now surrounded by six vases of beautiful flower arrangements and even two houseplants, which she loves. I thought of how happy she's going to be to take them home with her once she's released. One was ivy and the other a spider plant.

Haji was sitting in the chair but he had dozed off. I went back out to the nurse's station in a panic and asked where my grandmother's nurse, Sheila, was.

"I asked her to call me if any visitors came and she agreed but didn't follow through," I said to one of the ladies at the desk, basically the first one I laid eyes on.

Although I wanted to see the man in there, I wasn't ready yet and now I had been caught off guard. It was now five-thirty p.m. and I was told that there had been a shift change. Sheila was gone and they said she didn't give them those instructions before she left. Honestly, there was no point in me being upset with them. He was surely welcome to check up on her and had even come bearing gifts to lift her spirits. *How can I be mad at that?* Jax wasn't even that thoughtful and he's known her for most of his life.

I was only upset because I would have rather had the heads up that he would be here when I got back. I could have at least half-ass prepared myself for our meeting. I wasn't prepared

At All right now. I didn't know what I wanted to say to him or what he wanted to say to me.

"You know what, it's okay. The man in there is welcome to visit. I just needed a heads up, but – never mind, thank you," I said to the woman who now had a slightly confused look on her face.

I went back in to face the music. Of course he was now awake. He sat forward when I walked in the room with his forearms across his lap and his hands clasped and looked at me with what I thought was anger in his eyes. I didn't know how to take his glare so I just stood there, stuck in place, staring him in his eyes – hoping he could tell what they were saying, which was "I love you…Please don't me angry with me, but I'm hurt and confused, and not sure what do about this situation."

After what felt like ten minutes of silence, he got up and walked over to me. He is so handsome and looked so good – as he always does. He stretched out his arms for a hug and only then did my feet break free from the cement it felt like I was standing in. I melted in his arms, wrapping mine around his waist and pressing my face against his chest. We just held each other for a couple minutes until he stood back and put his hands on my shoulders and said, "Please don't ever do that again."

I knew what he meant – don't ever leave, ignore and avoid him for days like I had done.

"I won't, I promise," I responded as we embraced once again. My gram opened her eyes and smiled at us. She then looked around and her smile got wider. She looked at Haji, seeming to *know* they came from him and said "Thank You Sweetheart. You are such a gentleman."

How she know I didn't get the flowers and plants for her? I was a little jealous, but oh so happy to see her happy.

"Hey Ms. Lo, I'm glad you like them. You are more than welcome."

Ms. Lo? Since when they get so close to where he got a little pet name for her and stuff. I haven't been gone that damn long.

I put my hands on my hips and with a playful attitude I asked her, "And how you know I didn't buy the flowers Grandma? You just gon' give him all the credit?"

We all laughed and she responded, "Didn't you just come from the house. I have two new plants in my bedroom from him and two in the family room and two in the kitchen. He has been by to check on me every day since you've been gone and each time he came with plants, so I just assumed all this was his doing Sweetness. I know you love your ole' granny."

Sweetness was her lil nickname for me. I love when she called me that and it was a name that only she used.

Truth was I didn't even see my bedroom, let alone hers or the rest of the house when I went home. Leslie had seen me pull up and of course she wanted to know whose car I was driving.

She hollered out her door, "Damn Trick, been gone for a few days and come back driving a fly ass whip. Who shit you pushing?"

She had no discretion but I screamed back at her anyway, having none of my own, "The chick you see at the wheel hoe. Come check me out."

We hugged when she made her way across the street. She asked about my gram and helped me unload the car. We set my bags on the floor of the living room and I ended up going over to her house where we sat, smoked and talked for almost two hours. Of course we talked about Jax and our eventful few days together before I made my way back to the hospital to be with my gram.

Which brings us here and I felt like hiding under a rock. While I was in Maryland sexing my *friend,* this man been checking up on my gram daily and lifting her spirits. She loves plants and they are always the perfect gift to make her happy.

"Awe, that was very sweet of you," I said, looking up at Haji who was now standing up, on the opposite side of my grandmother's hospital bed - in the same spot Jax was standing only hours ago. I quickly let go of that thought because right now, I don't even want to think about him, especially not with Haji in the room. I was nervous enough as it were, knowing he wasn't going to leave my side tonight without *talking* and Jax will surely end up the topic of discussion. *I'm sure of it.* I'll cross that bridge when I get there.

I'm sure my grandma wanted to know about my trip, my new car and the details of all my activities while I was away, but since Haji was there, she waited. I wondered what she thought of the situation. She's not blind to what I have going on with either of these men and I'm sure she's wondering what the hell I done got myself into.

We all talked and laughed a while longer and I was feeling more at ease seeing her with so much energy. Visiting hours were over at eight o'clock and he had stayed with us the whole time, just like I knew he would. I guess he really was missing me, which was good because I missed him too. Before I took my four day hiatus, we were pretty much inseparable. But

145

that was before I knew about *her* and now I wasn't sure how things were going to go from here.

I kissed my gram and told her I'd stop in before I went to work in the morning and then I would come back and sit with her when I got off for the rest of the day.

"You don't have to babysit me child. Your ole' granny will be fine. Now, you go get *you* some rest and just make sure you call me and let me know you got home okay."

We have such a bond that I understood just from how she said it that she knew how uneasy I felt and that I had a lot on my mind. Boy does she have *No* idea the turmoil going on in my heart. I was afraid that Haji wouldn't feel the same once we left and I got in a car that another man had bought me. A man I had sex with three days ago – a day after *our* first time, but then again… I didn't know why. *Why am I so nervous*?! After all, he and I are no more of a couple than Jax and me, so it shouldn't really matter, Right?. *What's the big deal?* It is what it is.

We walked to the elevator holding hands and I wondered if he felt the shakiness in mine. I was happy to let go so that I could push the button to go down. The elevator was empty when we stepped on and as soon as the doors closed he asked me how I was getting around. I'm thinking, *Damn, here we go*!

"Haji, we need to talk."

Nervousness definitely took over and I couldn't look him in the eye. I pressed the button to take me to the garage floor that my car was on. He didn't bother to choose anything. He lifted my face up for me to look in his eyes.

"Okay. We'll talk. I'm coming with you, going wherever you're going so we can do just that. So my question

146

again is, are you riding with me or what? How are you getting around?"

It was as if he was asking a question he already knew the answer to the way he said it, or maybe I was just being paranoid. I sighed and shook my head side to side slowly and repeatedly.

"No what?" he asked, "What's wrong Nitra? Spit it out."

The doors opened up and we stepped off the elevator into the garage.

"Haj, listen, I'm going to be honest with you about everything, but right now I need you to know that I choose you and if you're truly getting a divorce, then I will think about giving us a chance."

He looked hurt and a little confused. All I could do was look away.

"What do you mean you *choose* me? There's someone else to choose from? And you still didn't answer my question. Look at me. Tell me what's up."

His expression changed, looking as though he had an epiphany and that light bulb went off in his head. The look in his eyes changed from confusion to showing a twinge of anger.

"Dude from the shop the day I started working there huh? The one you said wasn't competition, who was just a friend ... who you were adamant about no longer giving the benefits to... You fuck him Nitra? That's who you've been with these last several days? That's the "friend of the family" your grandma kept telling me you were with? Wow Nitra! This shit ain't cool." His hand was stroking his newly groomed beard and he kept shaking his head from side to side.

147

I didn't know what to say. I wasn't ready to deal with all of this right now.

"Why the fuck do you care? Mr. I-have-a-fucking-wife! You want to talk then let's just go. This isn't the time or place to be having this conversation so let's just go."

I put my free hand that wasn't holding my purse up to my forehead and closed my eyes. And I still have yet to reveal the damn car. This can't be life!

I have to drive out of this damn garage if we're going make it anywhere to talk about all this and of course he was now standing there looking at me with much disdain in his facial expression already, so I just let it out, "Yes, that's who I was with… and he bought me a car." I quickly added, "But you have to let me explain. This car is the least he could do for what he done to me while I was there. I'll explain later. Let's just go to your house so we can talk. I'll tell you everything."

Well, not everything…. He doesn't need to know I had sex with him. I'm cutting his ass off anyway so it won't be happening again. I can bet you that much.

He looked like he wanted to hit me, but something told me he was too much of a man to do it. I wanted us to go to his house because of all the packages I had dropped off hours earlier at mine - all the clothes and shoes and purses and things that I accumulated while with Jax were sitting right in the middle of the living room. I didn't get a chance to put anything away because Leslie and I went in the house, dropped the bags on the floor and left right back out to go to hers.

"You're not parking that shit in front of my house. Go drop it off, get some clothes and I'll be by to pick you up. My truck is on another floor. I'll meet you there."

148

He turned and walked away from me. I took note of the stride he had when he's angry, mad, hurt or whatever he was at the moment – but it was so sexy to me. "Maybe I should piss him off more often." I dismissed that thought quickly.

Nah, I'm not going to be toying with that man like that. Not to mention, he had a look in his eyes that said he was not to be fucked with. I picked up on that. It scared me a little, yet excited me a lot – at the same damn time. I could tell he wasn't perfect, but I think he's damn perfect for me. I'm sure I'll get to see his "I'm mad as Fuck" face again and the way he walks when he's angry and trying to get the hell away from me. That is, if tonight ends with us even being in a "Rela-friend-ship" as it were, let alone anything more.

We had never verbally made anything official, but we basically operated as a couple and have been inseparable for the last two months. Not a day passed that I didn't at least talk to him since I've met him until the night I found out he was married. He asked me to make it official that night but instead I ended up on a four day hiatus in Maryland with Jax. I couldn't do anything but stand here and shake my head. I let out a big sigh. Jax is going to have to let me go and I need to decide what I'm going to do about Haji.

For starters, I'm going to tell him the truth about how I feel tonight and if he still wants to be with me, all he has to do is say the right shit and I'm his.

I walked to my car, got in, adjusted my seat belt and headed home to pack an overnight bag. When I got there, I called myself parking across the street in front of Leslie's, as if I could hide it or something. I figured I'd at least try to soften the blow by not having it parked directly in front my house when he pulls up. He didn't bother or care to see it while we were at the parking garage or he would have walked me to it. He left my ass

149

standing there and walked off all sexy and angry and shit, so I'm guessing he didn't' want to see me get in it and drive off, or in it at all for that matter . I could dig it, but I also knew how I would respond if he asked me not to drive it, or worse, get rid of it. I needed it and I was keeping it.

After packing my bag, I sat outside on the porch with my Kindle while I waited. I made sure to pack one of my new set of sexy pajamas I brought back. Sure Jax bought it, but he wasn't the one who was going to see me in it.

I used the time that was passing to look at Facebook. My newsfeed was off the chain. I so wished they had other options instead of just to *like* a status. I would surely have taken the thumbs down approach on a lot of the bullshit I was reading as I scrolled down, but then again, I understood that people are who they are and more than likely were not going to change. I accepted that fact and it all became just funny to me. Hey, they were being true to themselves and I've come to expect nothing more or less.

I did, however, like a pic that Selena had posted earlier. Her caption read "Glowing". The first thing I thought when I saw that word was – *Pregnant*!

O.M.G – shit really gonna hit the fan between her and Carmen if she is. They going head to head for a spot in that man's heart and I can't wait to see how it all plays out in the end.

After waiting for about twenty more minutes, I started to think he wasn't coming. It didn't take that damn long to get from the hospital to my house. What, ten, fifteen minutes at the most? Shit, I'd been home for just about an hour now.

Just as I was about to get up and take my stuff back in the house, I saw his truck hit the bend, headed in my direction.

Butterflies danced around in the pit of my stomach as he pulled up in front of my house and parked.

He got out, leaving the engine running and came up on the porch, grabbing my bag. "Let's roll", he said, without any eye contact.

He opened up the passenger side door so I could get in like he always did. I got in and started to put on my seatbelt and he stood between me and the door.

"So, where's your car? Why it's not parked in front of your house?"

I know damn well he knows that's my car across the street. He's just being smart.

I nodded in the direction of Leslie's house. He turned around, looked at it, then back at me and slammed my door shut. He opened the back door and put my bag on the seat and slammed that one shut too. Making his way to the driver's side, I thought for sure an argument was coming, but to my surprise, he just pulled off, not saying a word. I guess he's going to wait until we get to his house to blow up on me.

He was quiet for a minute and then he asked me if I'd eaten anything. I told him I hadn't and was actually hungry. I had been running around all day and I guess I just forgot to eat, but these hunger pangs I'm feeling right now is telling me I've ignored them long enough.

I thought we were going to stop at a restaurant along the way, but he kept on trucking towards his house. We rode the rest of the way in silence, lost in our thoughts, I guess.

When we finally pulled up in front of his house, he parked but left the engine running as he got out coming around and opening my door. I hopped out the truck, noticing he was taking his house key off the ring of his keys.

"Go in and make yourself comfortable while I go grab us something to eat. I'll be right back."

Before I could protest and tell him I preferred to cook us something or at least ride with him, he had already made his way back to the driver's seat. I decided to go in and wait without making a scene.

What's Done In The Dark

Haj

Chelle had called when I was on my way to pick up Nitra. I told her I'd stop by on my way home, but of course with Nitra with me, I decided to drop her off at my house first and then head over. I wanted to know what was so damn urgent. Instead of picking up the food first, I went straight there because I wanted the food to still be hot when I got back to the crib.

I let myself in when I got there because technically, it is still *my* shit. I called out Chelle's name.

"I'm in here."

Her voice was coming from what used to be *our* bedroom. When I got to the entrance of the door, there she lay butt ass naked in the middle of the bed, legs stretched out wide with two fingers in her pussy and her other hand massaging her breasts. My dick instantly got hard and I was turned on at the sight of her sexy, raunchy ass. I hated the person she was but loved the freak in her. Oh, and she sucks my dick so well like only she can.

She knew what the fuck she was doing but I knew I couldn't do this shit with my boo at the crib hungry and waiting on me. I need to save my energy for her. This dick been wanting some more of that for days.

"See what I have to do since you don't love me anymore. I'm horny Haj. Technically that's still my dick, so let me get some," she said seductively between soft moans.

"Come on Chelle. Cut the bullshit. I didn't come over here for this."

She continued pleasing herself. My dick was still holding up a tent in my cargos. I grabbed it and held it while I continued to watch.

"What's so urgent that you couldn't talk over the phone?"

She sat up, still pushing her fingers in and out. Lifting her titty up, she started circling her nipple with her tongue.

"You play too damn much," I said, walking up closer to her.

She stood and I was directly in her face, so close that if I got any closer, we'd be kissing. Her lips are soft and her lip gloss added luster, creating a glow of what they'd look like if I came all over them juicy muh-fuckas. She leaned in to kiss me and I pulled back, still holding my dick. She replaced my hand with one of hers and used the other to unbuckle my belt.

"We're not fucking Chelle. In fact – I got to go. I don't have time for this shit. I'm not happy about this game you playing right now."

She had managed to pull my rod out through the hole of my boxers and immediately went to work on it. I couldn't stop her. The shit felt too good. I said Fuck It and decided to enjoy the shit. She was such a pro that five minutes later, I was lathering her lips, rubbing my dick back and forth across them, glossing them with my cum, just like I imagined just minutes ago. I watched some drip down her chin as she laid back and spread her legs. She wanted me to enter the ocean and ride the waves with the stiff board I carried between my legs.

Instead, I put my man's back behind the curtain and zipped and buttoned my pants back up.

"Damn Chelle. I can't even front. You give some of the best head ever. I gotta go though. And I'd advise you to not cry wolf ever again in the future. Those types of games don't fare well when it comes to business. And you should already know how I feel about games."

She sat up and swung her legs off the side of the bed, "You can't be serious right now! Oh, What? This new bitch must have your nose wide open. You never turned this pussy down before. And what – what am I supposed to do for sex while I'm pregnant with your child? Huh? I'm trying to be respectful. A bitch has needs. So what's it gonna be? What you wanna do?"

She had a point but I wasn't convinced she was really pregnant. And shit, we've been separated for two years, it could very well be somebody else's baby.

"I tell you what. You have a point, so this is what I'll do. I'll be by tomorrow morning with a pregnancy test. I want to see you take that shit in front of me."

She burrowed her brows and clenched her teeth, hopping up off the bed like she was ready to fight. I gave her that look and she sat her ass back down.

"Oh, so I'm a liar now? You don't believe me? Fine, what time you coming?"

"Fuck No, I don't believe you. And it doesn't matter what time. Just be ready to piss on the stick when I get here."

I walked out of the room and headed towards the door, "I'll holla."

She was on my heels, "You know that's fucked up right? But it's cool. See you tomorrow." She slammed the door as I walked out and down the steps to my truck.

I called in an order for our food and thought about my lil sweetheart waiting at the crib for me. Chelle was trying to be slick cause she think she know a nigga. I'm sure she can read me better than anyone else so she probably figured out that I'm digging girly…and she's right. She tried to entice me like she always does and usually I'd be with it just to get my shit off. Joke's on her ass though cause I had plans on putting my thing down on someone else tonight. She thought she was doing something but what she doesn't understand is none of the bitches she called herself chasing away before meant anything to me. They were just something to do, but Nitra – she's different, she's special.

I just couldn't pass on the head though – the shit was pleasurable and I was a sucker for a fierce slob of the knob. She grips and jiggles my handle like no other. Strong jaws, gag reflex, soft kisses, slurps and spit and slobber – the whole nine. Just thinking about it was getting my dick hard all over again. I wasn't far from pulling up to the food joint and I definitely wasn't walking in there looking like a perv, so I shook off those thoughts, gathering myself to make him stand down. I turned the music up and thought about Nitra for the rest of my drive.

Chelle

I stormed to the kitchen and made me a drink. I needed a stiff one to calm my nerves.

I went into the living room and plopped down on the love seat. I took my phone off the charger so I could call Kam. She answered on the third ring.

"Wassup Shelly, what's good?"

"Nothing, nothing's good," I said with attitude, "In fact, shit is all bad." I took a sip of my Henny and chased it with a Heineken.

"Well damn Bitch, you sound like you're all about to cry and shit. What the fuck happened? Who cut your horns and tail off, got your panties all in a bunch."

"Haj. That's who. And you're right – my panties are in a *dry* ass bunch and my breath smells like the cum that should be swimming in my fallopian tubes, racing to fertilize my damn egg."

I took another sip of my drink and my beer and lit up a Newport. I know I sound crazy, if not stupid, but I was hoping to get him to fuck me so that my chances of really being pregnant would rise. Instead there's zero percent chance because I swallowed the damn babies and the rest was used as lube for my lips.

Kam laughed at me, "What the fuck are you saying Shelly? You sound stupid as hell right now."

"I'm saying Haji was just here and instead of him fucking me and getting me knocked, he let me suck his dick and then tucked his shit away talking about he had to go. And that's not even it. The bigger problem is I told this mother fucker I was trying to be respectful by calling him over to get some instead of fucking another muh-fucka while I'm pregnant with his baby and you know what he had the nerve to say?"

157

"What?"

"He said I had a point but he doesn't believe I'm pregnant. So, he's coming over here in the morning with his own pregnancy test so I can piss on the stick in front of him."

"Ew Shit! I told you, you were crazy for even trying that one. Haj ain't stupid Shelly. So what you going to do now? You already know it's going to be negative, and then what?"

"I don't fucking know. Your ass need to bring me some of your sister's pee. Tell her I'll pay her or whatever."

"What? Bitch, you done lost your damn mind. Girl, you crazy! Me taking a picture of her positive keepsake pregnancy test is one thing, but I'm not about to ask my sister to piss in a cup for you. That's some ole' other shit and you know Karysma isn't going for that. She'd look at me like I had two necks."

"Come on Kam. If he finds out I'm lying tomorrow, he will kick me out on the street without a second thought. He already was pissed about me calling and saying it was urgent he come here when I was only trying to fuck. Talking bout I was crying wolf. He came over here thinking it was something important about business. If he finds out I'm not pregnant, he'll never trust me again. He'd consider that the ultimate crying wolf scenario and look at me in disgust."

"Well, that's your dumb ass fault for playing that game with him in the first place. You're too old to be doing this dumb shit anyway. I'll see what I can do, but I got company right now so bye Shelly."

She hung up in my ear. I took the rest of my drink down in one gulp. Hopefully the bitch pulls through for me or else I'm fucked. The money will freeze up if he finds out about this shit and I need to think of something and quick.

I couldn't help but to think his new bitch must be at his house and that's why he was rushing out of here. I know he doesn't give a fuck about me for real, let alone love me, but one thing I know for sure is he loves this pussy and the way I puts it down.

I decided to call his house phone just to see if the bitch answered and to my surprise she did – after my fourth time trying.

Nitra

Haj's house phone kept ringing and ringing and I started to think it was him calling back to back, wanting me to answer the phone for whatever reason. My phone died and was on the charger in the living room, so I was guessing he figured this was the next best way to get in touch with me. I decided to pick up.

"Hello."

"I take it Haj didn't make it back yet," the voice on the other end stated.

"Um, no he hasn't. May I ask who's calling and take a message for him?" I asked.

"Oh, you've talked to me before. You should know who this is. This is his wife and soon-to-be mother of his child and to answer your question, yes, you can take a message. Tell my husband I said I'll be waiting to finish that unfinished business tomorrow morning and I thank him for at least stopping by to let me taste my chocolate stick before he came back to chill with your boring ass."

I took my phone off my ear and looked at it, then put it back, "Excuse me? Boring, fuck you mean? You know what – whatever! Yea, I'll tell him." I wasn't about to argue with this bitch. I will however be cussing his ass out once he comes through that door.

"Well, I figured you must be boring if he made a pit stop pass my house to see me while your ass is sitting there looking stupid and waiting on him. And thank you for being so kind as to give him that message for me. I can hardly wait."

"Bitch Bye." I hung up in her face. Now I wanted to go home. I got up to get my phone out the other room. I made it from his room to the living room when I heard his key in the door.

I stood at the top of the steps with my hands on my hips and a "You's a Foul Mutha-Fucka" look on my face. He stopped in his tracks after closing the door and looking up at me.

"Damn Girl. What's good? Why you grilling me like that?" He started up the steps.

I moved out of his way as he made it to the top, folding my arms across my chest as he walked by me towards the kitchen

"Take me home. I don't know why I agreed to come over here in the first place."

He pulled two plates and two glasses out the cupboard and proceeded to take the food he'd bought out of the bag.

160

"Why Nitra? I went to get us something to eat and come back and now all of a sudden you're ready to go... You said you were hungry right?"

I went and stood against the counter in front of the sink. "Nigga, you must have been hungry for something else too. Your wife called. She said she'll be waiting to fuck you in the morning but thanked you for at least letting her suck your dick tonight."

Sure that wasn't what she had said *exactly*, but *basically*, that's what the fuck she said.

He let out a little chuckle and shook his head from side to side, spooning rice, cabbage, oxtails and a piece of cornbread onto each of our plates.

"Fuck outta here. You serious? That's exactly why I can't do that bitch no more. She lie too much. Now listen, I did go over there because she lied and said it was an emergency that couldn't be discussed over the phone. When I get there, the only emergency was that she was in heat – trying to get me to fuck her. She got mad when I cussed her stupid ass out about crying wolf – that's bad business. Come on now sweetheart. Why would I do some shit like that with your fine ass waiting here for me. You answered the phone and let her feed you the bullshit."

He sounded sincere and almost amused that I fell for it. Of course she's angry because he doesn't want to be with her so she's trying to cause problems so I will choose not to be with him. But then again, that doesn't mean he's not lying through his teeth with a straight face either.

I decided I'd give him the benefit of the doubt, plus I was hungry and the food was looking and smelling real good to me right now.

Little White Lies

Nitra

We both sat on the carpeted floor, eating from our plates on the coffee table while watching a movie. I couldn't focus because I kept wondering if me entertaining the idea of being his woman would be a big mistake on my part. I wasn't sure I was ready to deal with his simple bitch of a wife, who has already proven that she was going to be a problem as far as I was concerned.

"This shit good ain't it?" He asked, picking up his glass from the coaster, sipping on his iced green tea.

The food was good and I couldn't even front, "Mmmhm, this hit the spot. Thank you. I'm full too."

I got up to take my plate to the kitchen and wrap it up. I placed it in the refrigerator and went back to take a seat next to him while he finished up his food.

Soon as I sat down, my phone sang, "There goes my baaaby." I cringed, suddenly remembering that I was supposed to change that ringtone. He looked at me and I at him.

"Answer it," he said with his mouth full.

I got up to get my phone off the end table at the other end of the couch. By the time I picked it, I'd missed his call. I was relieved for the moment but of course he called right back. He was probably calling to tell me he'd made it home safely like he always does.

I answered, "Hey Jax, wassup, calling to say you made it?"

"Nah, actually I'm still here." My heart sank. "I saw a friend of mine and ended up here longer than intended. I want to see you before I dip. Where you at? I'm in front of your house. Your car is out here but you're not answering the door. I know you don't have that nigga up in there?"

I cut my eyes towards Haj who had stopped eating and was watching me intently.

"Um, Jax I'm not at home. My friend picked me up. I'll be back home tomorrow though."

Haj's brow shot up but at this point I don't know what the fuck for – we *are* just friends right now.

"Your friend who? And why didn't you drive your car? Why is it parked in front of Leslie's instead of yours?"

"Jax, not now please. That's none of your business. I'll call you tomorrow." Before he could say anything else, I hung up and powered my phone off.

Haji got up and took his plate in the kitchen. I heard him turn on the water. That meant he was washing his plate. I loved how disciplined he was. He was definitely neater than me and I hoped he never asked me to move in with him because I could already see an argument there. I wasn't trifling but I wasn't a neat freak at all to say the least and he most certainly is by my observation.

Instead of returning to join me back in the living room, he headed to his bedroom. I couldn't read him and didn't know whether to stay put or follow.

Haj

    I felt some kind of way for real. Instead of straight playing this dude to the left, I sensed she couldn't bring herself to do it to him like that. I wanted to go in on her about it, especially the fact his ringtone hasn't changed since the day we met.

    He called when we were introduced and her phone sang a song that said to me "You've Got Competition."

    Her beauty was captivating and I was drawn to her on sight. After rapping with her when I took her home that night, I knew I wanted her to be mine. Her head is on right, her conversation is intelligent – wise beyond her years, and she smelled good too. I love it when a woman smells good. The more time we spend together, the more I fall in love. I knew early that she was 'the one' – and that I'd wasted precious time and a ring on the wrong one the first time around. Shit, I knew I'd made a mistake a week after marrying Chelle, but I was in a state of mental transition, calling myself doing the right thing by my seed she was carrying so I tried my best to stick with it. I see now the folly in that decision. She ain't shit and just money hungry. What's done is done though and I am making some changes. Starting tonight.

    Instead of tripping about her lil phone call, I'd let it be her one and only pass. It's the least I can do considering I just came from getting some head from Chelle and lied about it. I don't even like referring to her as my wife – she's not worthy of the title, so she's just Chelle.

    A jealous feeling invaded my heart and I decided to take a shower to help me calm down. I washed my plate and headed to the shower in my bedroom without saying a word to Nitra as I walked by. I didn't want to say the wrong thing. I have a goal

164

and I'm not in the business of putting obstacles in my own way when I set out to achieve them.

I turned the water on, making sure it was steaming hot. The hamper in the corner of the bathroom became a makeshift basketball hoop as I got undressed and tossed my clothes in from where I stood.

I guess silence really is golden. Five minutes in and I had company. Nitra entered undetected, got undressed and joined me in the shower. She wrapped her arms around my waist from behind, laying her head on my back. Thirty seconds passed and I turned around and just stared in her eyes. We kissed and I wanted to give her the dick right then. I picked her up, turned around and placed her gently against the wall, the water spraying our bodies but sparing our faces. She wrapped her legs around my waist and I entered her with a long stroke, nice and slow. She closed her eyes and rocked her head from one side to the other while working her hips. Once I pushed in as far as I could go, I kissed her some more and just held him there in place as her walls closed in on him repeatedly. I knew when she had an orgasm and it turned me on that all I had to do was fill her up and it would cause her to ooze her sweet juices – enough to make a small puddle of sticky cum at our feet. I pulled out, wanting to move the show to the bedroom. We washed each other up before we took our show on the road.

There was no need for clothes or anything else. We were on each other like white on rice. It was on the minute we hit the bed.

Every time I pulled out, her pussy would contract. My dick felt like bait on a fishing pole and she was reeling me in. The shit was feeling so good but I wasn't ready to cum yet, so I pulled out, lifting her legs up over my shoulders and plunged my tongue deep into her gate of passion. I spelled my name with my

165

tongue up in her about ten times and she was calling it out as I did. I stopped and came up to kiss her so she could taste her own sweetness, while sliding back up in her at the same time. I slid my tongue in her mouth as we clasped our fingers together, moving in and out of her – speeding up, and then slowing down.

"Be my woman Nitra." I told her in between breaths. "I want this all to myself. Be mine, Sweetness."

Her grandma had called her that earlier. I'm making that my name for her too – we just have two different meanings. Ms. Lo doesn't have to know that when I say it – it's sexual.

"Okay. I'm all yours."

She was panting and on the verge of her third orgasm and I couldn't hold mine any longer. We exploded almost in unison and I laid there on top of her, never pulling out. I was spent – and I'm sure she is too!

She started messaging my head and the shit was feeling good.

"So it's official – you're mine? I got you all to myself?"

"Yes Baby, I'm all yours."

"Well then I can expect that when you talk to ole' boy tomorrow that you're going to let him know." It was a statement, more than a question.

"Yes, I will call him and let him know."

"Bet. Goodnight Baby. You got me spent."

"Likewise Baby. Goodnight."

We repositioned ourselves and she was now laying on my chest with one of her legs sprawled over mine.

"Nitra, one more thing. We don't have to even get in to everything. I just need to ask you something. Did you sleep with him while you were gone?" I had to ask.

Just above a whisper, she answered, "No. He hit me. That's why he bought the car. He knew I slept with you and became angry. That was his way of apologizing."

"Wow. That's some bitch shit. Look at me for a second." She lifted her head and looked in my eyes. "I promise to never put my hands on you. You hear me? That's my word."

"Okay."

"Tomorrow I want you to tell that nigga to fuck off. You got a real man in your life now. You hear me?"

"Yes, I hear you. And I believe you. He's cut off – and I will tell him tomorrow, now let's go to bed. I'm exhausted."

"Goodnight."

"Goodnight Love."

It felt good to hear her call me that. If she wasn't in love yet, she will be.

I slept good. I thought about the possibility that I'd just planted my seed in her and I was happy to know I could be sure it was mine, should that be the case. I get the feeling she wouldn't lie to me about something like that. She has no need to.

Let the Games Begin

Chelle

When I woke up in the morning, the first thing I did was roll over and call Kam. When she didn't answer, I decided it was still early and she was probably still sleeping. The shower was calling my name and I intended to answer immediately.

When I got out, I called Kam again. She still didn't answer. I was starting to get nervous and thought that perhaps Karysma said "Hell to the naw." At nine thirty I texted Haji to see what time he was coming; trying to see how much time I had to come up with a Plan B.

Twenty minutes passed and he text me back: Be there in a minute. I was shitting bricks. I called Kam back four more times until I finally gave up and accepted my fate. Haji was going to be here shortly and he would find out that I lied about being pregnant. *Fuck My Life*!

Kam

This bitch must be out her damn mind calling me this early with her bullshit. I'm not getting in this mess. Haj ain't bout to put money on my head for aiding Chelle's stupid ass with this bullshit. Uh-uh. She's on her own with this one. I got more important things to do, such as this sexy specimen of a man lying next to me in my bed. He fucked me good last night.

He left afterwards, supposed to be on his way back home. He said he was hitting the road as soon as he left but ended up coming back about an hour later, saying there was a

168

change in plans. We fucked again and that time he fucked me like he was letting out some frustration on my ass.

He informed me this morning that five-o took a friend of his to jail last night. He needed me to ride with him to pick up his friend's car and follow him so he could drop it off. It was parked in front of some broad named Leslie's house where my boo gets his hair braided. I showered and got dressed so I'd be ready when he was.

Nitra

I couldn't wait to get to work so I could corner MaKenzie in her office to talk about my dilemma. I felt bad for lying to Haj last night but I planned on cutting Jax loose for good today anyway so I figured what he doesn't know won't hurt him. It was one little white lie.

Haji and I had sex for the second time last night without protection and I am convinced he wants me to have his baby. I only hoped it didn't happen just yet so I could be sure it was his when it did. I wasn't ready for any children yet no how.

If it happened now, I couldn't be a hundred percent on whether it was Haji's or if the baby belonged to Jax. Lord knows I don't want to go through that drama. I am so mad at myself but fuck it. Jax is history after today.

Pulling out my phone, I changed his ringtone to a generic one that was already pre-loaded on my phone – nothing special.

I got showered and dressed and Haj took me to work. On the way there, I called my grandma to let her know I'd be there after work to spend some time with her. She was sounding better over the phone and my heart was happy for that. I can't

169

wait to sit and talk with her. I plan to fill her in on some of the missing information I've been withholding from her and see what she has to say. I sucked up her wisdom like a sponge whenever we talked.

Haj

I dropped my baby off at work. My mission was accomplished – she was all mine and we made plans to see each other later.

I stopped at Rite-Aid on my way to Chelle and grabbed a box with two pregnancy tests. I was going to make her piss on both of them too.

Chelle

"I need a fucking drink," I screamed at the air.

I called Kam a total of nine times and she never answered any of my calls. I heard the door close and my heart fell to the floor knowing it was show time. I put on my game face and left the bedroom to face the music.

I walked in the living room to find Haj sitting on the sofa, looking delicious as usual – sporting a black Ralph Lauren shirt with a whit polo sign, some black cargo shorts and some black and white J's.

He held up a bag, letting me know he meant business. He stood up and led the way to the bathroom as I followed slowly behind.

"Can I have some privacy please?" I asked because he had took up residence on top of the sink.

170

"I don't think so Boo. You won't be tampering with the results or no shit like that. You might have somebody else's pee up in here with ya simple ass," he had the nerve to say as he jumped down and started opening the doors to the closet and the medicine cabinet.

I put my hands on my hip and cocked my head to the side, "You can't be serious right now?" I knew he was. I was trying to stall.

"Do what you gotta do," he said, taking a seat on top of the sink again.

"*Here goes the end of my world*," I thought to myself as I opened the box.

"Open em' both."

I looked at him like he was crazy, "For what? Are you saying you want me to take both tests?"

"That's right. That's exactly what I'm saying. You can never be too sure right?" He folded his hands, placing his forearms in his lap while he watched me.

I did as he said – hesitantly. I sat on the toilet holding both tests in my hand. Seconds later a stream of piss came flowing from my vagina like I'd had two gallons of water before he got here. I peed enough to use both. Placing them on the counter of the sink right next to him, I walked out of the bathroom to the living room and sat on the couch, waiting for confirmation of my doom. He came in and sat across from me, staring me in my eyes, neither of us saying a word. I was going over in my head what I was going to say when the test confirmed I wasn't pregnant. I kept coming up empty with any type of logical explanation. I started feeling dizzy and light headed.

171

A few more minutes of silence passed by and I watched him walk to the bathroom to retrieve the tests. He came back with both of them in hand and I was unable to read his expression. He handed them to me and my heart sank when I saw two pink lines on each of them, indicating that I was indeed pregnant. *What the fuck!*

I instantly felt nauseated and sick to my stomach, taking off running to the bathroom to spit up. He brought me some cold water and a cold rag. I took a sip of the water and then wiped my face, holding the rag in place for at least ten seconds. I was going through a thing and had to regain my composure. I let out a couple tears on that rag before I removed it.

He stood there just looking at me. I pulled myself together and brushed my teeth. I looked at him through the mirror and said, "So, now that it's confirmed, can I get some dick." I got right to the point.

"I shouldn't give you shit for that stunt you pulled last night. But – I'll make a deal with you though. I'll give you the dick as long as you don't start no shit with my girl. Nitra is my woman now Chelle and I don't want you bringing any drama her way. Deal?"

I turned around and stood face to face with him, "Really Haj? I'm still your wife and right now I'm pregnant. I know shit is fucked up but we can work on that."

It hurt to hear him tell me he had a woman while I was technically still his wife. Okay, so I claim to not love him but that was only because I knew he wasn't marrying me because he *loved me* in the first place. I have mad love *for* him and we will always share a bond – even if our son didn't make it.

"We've been separated for two years Chelle. Don't you think it's about time we cut the bullshit?"

"Well, maybe I would agree if you weren't leading me on. You still fuck me whenever I want it and I'm supposed to believe you're through. I'm pregnant Haj! Can't we at least try one more time? Let's give this baby a family. I promise I won't do any stupid shit like before."

Tears began to well up in my eyes. I went to the room and he followed. Truth is, I didn't want him for real, I just don't want any other bitch to have him either.

"I can't do that Chelle. I'm really feeling her. I can't hurt her like that. We just made it official. I'm going to take care of you and my child – you know that. But I want a divorce."

With tears streaming down my face, I started to undress. I could win an Oscar for this performance I was putting on.

"Okay fine. If that's what you want then that's what you'll get."

I laid back and opened my legs wide, inviting him to my pussy. He took his pants off, fucked me real good and left. That was cool though – I got what I wanted.

This was totally unexpected. I was shocked to find out I was really pregnant and I needed to make an appointment to find out how far along ASAP.

Unbeknownst to Haj, I've been fucking around with this guy name Stunna, well Sean, for the last seven months. Problem is, he went to jail over a month and a half ago. That's part of the reason I'm so pressed on keeping Haj in my pocket, cause mine is hurting. Since my man been in jail, the money I make

173

cleaning for Haj isn't enough to support my lifestyle. If I'm two months or more, this baby is definitely Stunna's, but if I'm only a month or so, it's definitely Haji's. Besides today, last month was the last time we had sex. I call him every now and then for some so he doesn't cut me all the way off and simply because I can never get enough of that anaconda swinging between his legs.

I made a call to my Gyne to make an appointment so I can find out for sure whose fucking baby I'm carrying. My next steps depend heavily on that information. I really didn't want to be a mother, but if a child can help keep my account full, I'd have one for that reason only.

It's Over...For Real This Time

Haj

I opened the door to let my partner in. He usually lay low unless he's handling his business but I needed my right hand to come out of hiding and lend a brutha his ear. I felt the need to lay this shit in his lap and see what he thought about all of it.

"What's good Bro…?" I dapped him up as he stepped through the door. He came in and we took a seat in the living room.

"So wassup my brutha… You sounded like you got some major shit going on when you called. I need to knock some fools off or what?"

I had to laugh. This dude here is never chillin'. Always ready and willing to pop off. A real live wire, that guy.

"Nah man. Muh-fuckas ain't stupid. I ain't having those type of problems. Although – I do see one bull in particular being a problem. Can you believe I done fucked around and fell in love?"

"What nigga? You called me over here cause yo ass is in love? And you bout to have drama with some cat about her? …You sucker for love ass nigga. Or what? You and Chelle decide to work shit out? She crazy but she's not that ba…"

Before he had a chance to finish his sentence, I cut his ass off, "Fuck No! I'm don't want her fam. And I'm not in love with her – never been. The fucked up thing is she's pregnant though. I just came from making her grimy ass piss on not one, but two sticks in front of me and both those muh-fuckas came

175

back positive. I'm mad as fuck for real. You know I was planning on divorcing her ass and now this shit. It's not gonna stop me though. Nitra is going to be pissed. Shit, I'm pissed – I want *her* to have my babies."

"I know you got something strong to drink up in here." He asked before responding to what I'd said.

I got up to grab us a bottle of Henny and a couple of beers.

"Damn Bro. Aye, you sure it's your seed she's carrying? You know Chelle raw. Nitra must be the new-new…"

"Hell no, I'm not sure. She think I don't know about the boy Sean. She been messing with him for some time now. I don't give a fuck so I never let her know that I knew about them. A blood test is certain as soon as it's born, that's for sure. And yea, Nitra – that's my Sweetness. She's young with an old soul and a good head on her shoulders – nothing like Chelle. I don't know how I fucked up and dealt with her simple ass man. I was blind-sided. Matter of fact – it's your fault nigga. For one, you the reason I met her. And two, you should have stopped me from fucking with that train wreck. You knew what type of bitch she was before I did."

He laughed at me. "HaHaaaa, Please… You a grown ass man dog. That was your choice and your choice alone. And ain't nobody tell you to wife her ass – that was definitely all you with that suddenly wanting to walk the straight and narrow bullshit you were on at the time." HA! – He laughed out loud, "Look what that got your ass."

"Fuck you! But you right. That was bad business on my part. Total lapse in judgment. Knowing her, she gone use this pregnancy shit to try to cause problems. She already conning ya

176

boy into giving her the dick, talking bout she don't want to disrespect me by fucking another dude while my seed up in her. The crazy part is I plunged so deep into my new boo last night that she could quite possibly be telling me the same thing soon."

"Damn Homie. Don't you think you're moving a little fast with this new broad?"

"Nah Vaughn, she's the one. I'm telling you V. Trust me, I'd never make the same mistake twice. There's just something about her man. She got my nose open bruh and you know I don't be checking for none of these hoes out here like that."

"If you say so man. How old is she?"

"Twenty-two. Birthday in November."

He threw his hands up in the air, "Awe man, she's a baby homie. She still got a lot of growing up to do and you talking bout she's the one. Is she even out of training bras yet?"

"Ha-ha! Fuck outta here. She's beyond legal and I'm telling you man, she's on some other shit. She's a nail tech at that upscale spot call MAD Styles. She has goals and shit, aspiring to open up her own shop one day. I'ma help her do that shit too."

I noticed he shifted in his seat and was now wearing a serious expression.

"What's up guy – you look like you just spaced out. Where you at?"

"MAD Styles." He repeated the name of Nitra's job.

"Yea. It's nice up in there. I took over the cleaning contract for the building. You know Greg, the barber who cuts my hair at his crib?" He shook his head yes. "Yea, he used to do it but he got a new nighttime gig and put me on. That's how I met her. Girly that own the spot's husband is a cool dude. He just got some sneaky ass eyes. Always look like he up to something."

He took a gulp of the Henny and began to speak. "Yea, the nigga is sneaky and that sneaky shit led his wife right into my arms."

My eyes got big and I almost spit out the liquor from the shot I'd just taken. I couldn't believe what I was hearing. *Small fucking world.*

"What did you just say? Since when?"

"Bout six months now. Dig this shit – the nigga is fucking one of the stylist bitches that work at MaKenzie's shop. His dumb ass don't even know she knows. She got some shit planned for the both of them and once she carries it out, she'll be all mine. Her shit will still be MAD Styles, but I'm gonna change her name to Dahlson instead of Dixon. MaKenzie Antoinette Dahlson – I like the sound of that. Now her bro, she's a bad bitch. Matter of fact, I can't even disrespect her like that. She's my angel. Far from a bitch."

He must have been trying to read the expression on my face.

"Don't judge her man. She's a good girl who deserves better. The nigga is wild, I'm telling you. You wouldn't believe the shit she has on him. I'm going to marry her Haj. I just might pull one of your moves. Only she's not a hood chick like Chelle.

I'd quit the game for her man. Just like you was trying to do. Just gotta know they worth it man."

"Right, right. Damn, it's like that? And you in here calling me a sucka for love. You got your nerve – *you* talking about quitting the game and marriage and shit. Wow!"

We rapped for a lil while longer. It felt good to get some of this off my chest and he was the only cat I'd talk to on some personal shit.

Good thing I wasn't interested in being friends with the boy Reese – we kept everything strictly business and only talked when it was time to deal with the cash.

I told him about the boy Jax. I could tell that dude was one to watch closely and we ain't had two words yet. If he is as fucked up about girly as I am, I'd have to reduce his days on this earth if he got in my way. She's mine now, which means she's off limits.

He reminded me about the gambling convention that was coming up next month on September 4th. Only two were held per year and nothing but the big dogs would be in attendance, as well as some with a little less bank, trying to get their weight up. Guaranteed millions stood to be in the building and guns weren't allowed in. They even had maximum security that patrolled the inside and outside – making sure no one came to stick up the joint. No one could enter or exit at the same time unless it was people who came together. It was a move to ensure the winners would make it home with their gwop – well at least make it to their whip and off the lot without the losers setting the guns ablaze before you even had a chance to make it to your ride. Getting home safely – and alive - was your problem once you were off the property and it was a chance many men chose to take – all about that money.

Nitra

I was on time when I got to the shop but not as early as I usually am. Haj wore my ass out last night. Surprisingly as I walked in the door, everybody was there…well, except for Selena, but that's nothing new as of late. I noticed MaKenzie's door was shut as I walked in. I greeted everyone who was busy working on their clients already. It was normally busy from open to close and we already had a full house.

Since I went on a four day impromptu vacay, I didn't have anyone scheduled. I was very anxious to talk to MaKenzie so I buzzed her line from the phone at my station.

"What's up sweetie pie? Get your butt in here?"

She must have been just as anxious to talk to me as I was her. I went in her office and shut the door.

"Heyyyy! So, what's new?"

"Unh-uh. We'll talk about me in a minute. What's new with *you*," she was pointing her cell phone at me that was in her hand.

"Well – we talked and long story short – he's officially my man now." I let a big cheesy ass grin spread across my face.

She squealed, "Yes! I'm happy for you girl. That man adores you. That's really good news. Pretty soon we'll be planning yall's wedding."

"Whoa, whoa, whoa – not so fast sistah! Marriage isn't in our forecast just yet. He still has to get a divorce first remember?"

"Yea, Yea – that's still gon' be your husband. I can tell. He was like a sick lil puppy around here while you were gone. Speaking of which – spill it!"

I ran everything down about my days spent with Jax and filled her in on everything in between leading up to us meeting right this moment. Needless to say, she was speechless.

"Girl, I don't know what to say. You've had quite an eventful few days."

"Tell me about it."

My phone started to ring. "Because I got high" was singing, letting me know it was my neighbor, Leslie. *What the hell she want this early?*

"Wassup ma'am, what you doing up so early?" I answered.

"Girl, Jax done brought some broad over here and they about to drive off with your car."

"What?"

"Some brownskin chick with braids. I know this broad from somewhere too – I just can't put my finger on it. But yea, she looking all stank with the shortest, tightest booty shorts ever made – looking like a walking yeast infection waiting to happen. He got the nerve to be giving her your keys so she can drive your car girl. What the hell you done did to him? He's crazy about you. You must have pissed him off something serious." She was talking a mile a minute.

"Uuuugh, I'm so mad right now. That's his fucking problem – he's crazy – not just about me either – he's just one crazy mutha-fucka. Thanks Les but let me call you back."

181

I immediately dialed Jax. He picked up on the second ring.

"Somehow I knew you'd be calling me. That was quick. I haven't even pulled off yet and Les done called you already. Fuck you want anyway?"

"You know what – I'm glad you just pulled this bullshit. You make shit so fucking easy for me. Take that stinking ass car and don't say shit else to me. I'm sure my man will be happy it's gone. I'll have some new shit in no time. Fuck you Jax! It's over – for real this time! Lose my number." I was too through on that one. Kenzie just sat there shaking her head.

"Girrrrl, what you gon' do with him? He crazy as hell! He wild as hell for that."

"Nothing. I'm not doing anything with him. We're done! He just made this shit that much easier."

September 4th - About to go down...

Nitra

Today was a big day for MaKenzie and an even bigger one for Nel and her sister Autumn. Their wedding day had finally come.

Things were going well with Haj and I was so happy to have him as my own. He treated me so special – always, making me feel like I was the most beautiful woman in the world – daily. He replaced my car the very next day after Jax pulled his little stunt. I haven't heard from him since and I was truly happy about it. *Less drama this way*!

I was floored when Haj showed up at my house in a rose colored Audi with my name personalized on the licensed plate. I loved my new car and I smiled at the thought of pulling up to the wedding in style in my own shit.

I was in my room trying to get ready, zipping around trying to hurry up. The wedding was to start in a little over an hour and I hadn't even showered yet. At least my hair, nails and toes were already on point.

I was looking forward to having a good time and spending the night with my man afterwards, but I couldn't help but feel a little disappointed that he was opting to go to some gambling convention, instead of attending the wedding with me. It was all good though. My understanding is he stood to gain a lot of money and the opportunity only came a couple times a year. For him, gambling was a hobby more than an addiction so I never worried about him losing and neither did he. However, he is one who plays to win at all times and I was certain we'd be sleeping on big faced bills tonight.

My gram has been doing really well since her hospital stay and she was actually getting out of the house to go to the thrift store with one of her old lady friends. She loves Haj. She knew all about his situation but never doubted his love for me; however she made it a point to ask him about his impending divorce every chance she got.

I put some pep in my step so I could make it to the wedding on time. I wasn't about to miss this. I love weddings! I couldn't wait to eat, drink, dance and share in the special moment with the love birds. Even though Nel and I did what we did, I was really, really happy for the two of them and knew it would never happen again.

Selena

I wasn't looking forward to seeing Reese and MaKenzie looking all happy together at the wedding. I really didn't want to go, but I actually liked Autumn. Nel was cool peoples too and the whole shop was invited to attend.

I decided to go, contemplating on rather I had the balls to tell MaKenzie about the baby I'm having with her husband on her sister's wedding day or not. I'm pissed because he still hasn't told her and he's known for quite some time now. Initially, I thought he was going to break wide and move his whole family to another state the way he acted when I first broke the news. I didn't speak with him for a couple days at first and then he called me wanting to talk. He promised to take care of the baby but made me promise in return to let him handle things on his own terms. I agreed, but was growing increasingly irritated with getting her sloppy seconds. He called himself breaking things off with me the night I told him but I guess the news made him change his mind. Things aren't the same between us but he is very attentive to my growing belly bump.

184

I'm now four months pregnant and can't wait until my shop is done in a couple more months so I can be free of even seeing her face. Once I'm out of there, I'm pretty sure I won't be holding it in much longer – there would be no need to. I'd be out of the danger zone per se.

It was to the point I couldn't hide it anymore if I wanted to anyway, so I decided to stop trying. I was already starting to show, so today I chose a dress that would leave no question – purposely. If I have to be uncomfortable all day, so will he.

I headed out the door so I can get this damn day over with. *Lord, give me strength!*

Maurice

The wedding was set to begin. Everyone was in their respective positions and I was ready to enjoy myself for a change. All I know is work and tonight I get to play a little. We were all standing in the hallway about to begin the ceremony when the doors to the church opened and in a walked a visibly pregnant Selena. My stomach instantly started turning in knots.

I managed to avoid the scenario of being around the two of them at the same time until today and the shit had my palms sweaty as hell.

She looked cute and comfortable and I couldn't take my eyes off her stomach as she walked pass and her ass as she made her way inside to take her seat. *That Ass!* I looked at my wife who was standing across from me, seemingly oblivious to the glances Selena and I stole with one another when she came through. She was more fixated on the growing waistline that showed through Lena's outfit like everyone else. I was nervous as hell and was beginning to think tonight wouldn't be an enjoyable one after all. I kept feeling like all eyes were on me.

The music began and we did our thing. Kenzie and I were paired together. I was Nel's best man and she was the Maid of Honor. We went down first and then the rest of the wedding party followed suit as rehearsed.

The whole ceremony was beautiful – Nel outdid himself on this one. It didn't get any better than this and I'm sure his new wife was the happiest woman alive right now. I was truly taken aback, tears all in my eyes and shit and knew I had to get real creative to top this one once me and my baby's day came along. My heart sank as I stole another look at Selena, all while hoping Kenzie and I even made it that far.

Haj

I picked up Vaughn so we could ride together to the Gambler's Convention. We decided since both our ladies' would be tied up celebrating with the newlyweds all night that we'd go do a little celebrating of our own. I let him talk me into some shit and I was already beginning to regret my decision to go along with it.

Due to the nature of his profession, Vaughn didn't do crowds, so he decided to throw his own lil private party after we were done at the convention. I knew what that meant and it all boiled down to - *Trouble!*

We decided we would stay until we were either up or down a hundred stacks – however long it took and then we was the fuck out of there. That was chump change to us so it didn't matter either way. We saw it as an opportunity to flip that shit and turn it into more, but if we didn't, whatever – it was just something to do. There were only two outcomes when it came to this gambling shit with us – we either win big, or lose small. Money just isn't an issue for us. We consider gambling more of

a hobby rather than an addiction. We gon' be good either way –
win or lose.

If there is such a thing as luck, it was definitely on our
side tonight. We went in there lightning shit up. We were on
fire, hitting numbers playing craps – the game where the real
money was on the table. We even won three games of Dominos
a piece, worth fifty thousand a game. We left a trail of smoke
leaving out of there – most of it coming out of niggas ears – mad
as hell we came up like that in a matter of two hours. We were
way over quota and it didn't take no time to get it. *That's what
the fuck I'm talking about!*

We saw the mean mugs and ice grills – but they knew
better to try us. We got up out of there and stopped at some
rinky dink ass bar and threw a couple shots back to celebrate our
success for tonight. Without counting, I estimated we hit em' for
a good 1.5 million in two fucking hours. A few high price side
bets definitely added to our fortune. Niggas throw money
around like it's nothing up in there.

"Cheers" – Clink!

"Toast to the Get Money Boys… Remember that shit?
G-M-B all day!" V was clapping his hands and shit, cracking
the fuck up. He was in a very good mood and you could tell he
was starting to feel them shots and so was I.

I looked down at my watch. It was only ten-thirty and
we were hit. I started thinking about my baby and got a sudden
urge to see her. I wanted to kiss her. That's all. Real quick. I
pulled out my phone and looked at the picture she texted me
earlier of her in her dress she wore to the wedding. That did it. I
had to see her right quick. She was looking good as fuck!

"Yo V, I'm bout to swing by the reception so I can see my girl real quick. Fucking with you, I'm gon' be out all night. I'm gonna give her my key. I want her sexy ass at my house, in my bed waiting on me once we done for the night."

"Aye… Do what you gotta do bruh. I'm wit' it."

The look I saw in his eye should have been enough to change my mind about this, but I didn't. I drove clear across town to surprise my baby with a kiss.

We pulled up to the banquet hall where the reception was taking place. I knew the location because I was actually invited to attend as Nitra's guest but I opted to go to the convention instead. Nitra was starting to like spending money so she was cool with it. That's another thing I loved about her so much. She made my dick hard, but not my life.

I parked my truck and hopped out to make a quick appearance and extend my congrats to the newlyweds. I told bro I'd be right back and this dude gets out with me.

"I'm coming with you. You ain't staying right? We just dropping in and dropping out. What's the harm in that? I want to see my baby too, shit – just to see her in her dress."

"Don't you think that's a lil bit risky man? You know ole boy up in here. You bout to catch her off guard."

"That's exactly what I want to do. Let's go, cause I'm not getting back in that truck. You know it's an argument you're not gonna win so quit wasting precious fucking time."

I sighed, hoping I wasn't going to regret this later.

We went through a set of doors and was instantly put on the spot. Those doors were a direct entrance to the hall itself and all eyes were on us. My baby noticed me first.

"Babyyyyy." She squealed running over to hug me. The heels she had on in the picture she sent me had been replaced with some flats. She must have been partying hard cause her hair was starting to sweat out. She still looked beautiful and I did what I came to do and gave her a passionate kiss her on the lips.

I never shared with her the information Vaughn had shared with me about MaKenzie so she had no reason to be alarmed by Vaughn's presence. She was used to him stopping by the crib and they were actually getting cool. You'd think they've know each other their whole lives. We pulled our lips apart and she turned to greet him.

"Hey V... What's up bruh?" She looked to me and said, "This is a nice surprise. Come on yall, come say congratulations to the bride and groom."

Before I could say anything, she was pulling both of us by our wrists, headed right to a table where MaKenzie, her husband, the bride and groom and the rest of the wedding party were sitting.

We made it to the table and I shook Nel's hand while telling him and his new bride, "Congratulations! Today is the first day of the rest of your lives that you will be blessed to spend together... Make em' good and make em' count." I acknowledged the rest of the table, "How's everybody doing? Look like yall enjoying yourselves. Yall jamming up in here."

I couldn't help but notice the look MaKenzie was giving Vaughn. She couldn't help herself. Even I could tell she saw something she liked. This dude had the nerve to be looking her right in her eyes as well. *Are they fucking crazy!* I thought I saw hearts in them muh-fucka's eyes the way they were staring at each other.

I didn't know what to say so I just introduced the stranger in the room.

"Everybody this is my right hand, V."

Everybody spoke except for Reese. He had tunnel vision and was giving his wife the look of death right now. It was obvious I needed to get V the fuck out of there before shit got ugly.

Reese stood up abruptly with much anger in his eyes. He began to raise his voice at MaKenzie…

"Let me holla at you," he said through clenched teeth, "NOW!" He then turned and looked at Vaughn and pointed in the direction of the exit, "And you get the fuck up outta here before there be some serious shit up in here."

"What? Fuck is you talking to like that guy? You don't know me!"

V had that look in his eyes. It was about to go down up in this bitch….

THE END FOR NOW….

Find out what happens next when the sequel drops. I hope you enjoyed the read. Thank you for checking it out! This is my debut novel and the first installment of what I call "The Desire Series" – Stay Tuned!

© 2013 Author: Gina Camp

www.ingramcontent.com/pod-product-compliance
Lightning Source LLC
Chambersburg PA
CBHW070022260626
47159CB00005B/1925